"What did you do?" he growled.

Her jaw dropped as words failed her. Sweet Maka, help her. What *had* she done? In his dream, he was so handsome, so giving. The temptation and promise of anonymity were too much to resist, and she had lowered her guard.

"Oh, Great Spirit," she whispered.

"You invaded my dream."

"I never thought that... I mean, I didn't intend..." How could she finish? "Nicholas, please." She needed to recall who he was, no, *what* he was. But her body still trembled from his lovemaking.

"You really had me fooled, all aloof on the exterior, but oh, how you burn underneath...."

Books by Jenna Kernan

Nocturne

Dream Stalker #78
Ghost Stalker #111

*The Trackers

JENNA KERNAN

writes fast-paced romantic adventures set in out-of-the-way places and populated with larger-than-life characters.

Happily married to her college sweetheart, Jenna shares a love of the outdoors with her husband. The couple enjoys treasure hunting all over the country, searching for natural gold nuggets and precious and semiprecious stones.

Jenna has been nominated for two RITA® Awards for her Western historicals and is a popular speaker at writing conferences. Visit Jenna at her internet home, www.jennakernan.com.

GHOST STALKER

JENNA KERNAN

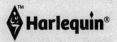

TORONTO NEW YORK LONDON
AMSTERDAM PARIS SYDNEY HAMBURG
STOCKHOLM ATHENS TOKYO MILAN MADRID
PRAGUE WARSAW BUDAPEST AUCKLAND

Recycling programs
for this product may
not exist in your area.

ISBN-13: 978-0-373-61858-3

GHOST STALKER

www.Harlequin.com

Printed in U.S.A.

Dear Reader,

This is my second paranormal romance in
The Trackers series, featuring Native American
shapeshifters called Skinwalkers. Their world is
full of dark and dangerous creatures with ancient
powers and is loosely based on Lakota myth.

I hope you fall in love with Jessie and Nick. Their
love will be tested and their lives endangered as
they struggle to protect the Seer of Souls from her
enemies and fight the Ruler of Ghosts for control
of the living world.

For more about Nick and Jessie and for a sneak
peek at my third in The Trackers series, please visit
me at my web home, www.jennakernan.com.

Jenna Kernan

To Amy,
who has long known how to walk in dreams.

Prologue

Nagi, ruler of Ghosts, spun in a circle of shimmering silver light, creating one bright spot in his tedious world of ceaselessly spiraling specters. Not all his subjects surrounded him as they should. Many still walked the earth, uncollected, awaiting his summons. His secret army.

Soon they would fight the Halfling defenders for supremacy. As immortals, his ghosts had the advantage. The important thing was to maintain the element of surprise.

To do that, he needed to kill that Seer. He could wait no longer. The threat was about to triple, for the Seer carried twins. She and her offspring were the only beings on the planet who could see his ghosts. He wanted no witness to their rising. His last attempt on her had failed. He'd underestimated her. She'd been clever enough to enlist the help of a troublesome Skinwalker, now her mate, and they'd undermined his ability to track her.

However, he had devised another way. Her mate had healing powers and he was never far from the Seer. But Nagi's invisible army were already scouring the earth for the wolf or the raven. Either could lead him to the Healer. Nagi would go himself, but there were more important matters only he could solve.

Nagi glowed brighter at the thought, causing a pitiful moan from the ghosts as they shrank back in torment. *Soon,* he thought, *soon I will strike!*

Chapter 1

Nicholas Chien searched the popular nightclub for the one who hunted him. A hunter himself, he knew the feeling of being stalked. Unlike the humans surrounding him, he paid close attention to his instincts. After all, they had kept him alive for over a century.

His eyes locked onto a woman who watched with the intensity of a falcon. His gaze flicked to her right and then left, recognizing the pack of three females—all with their attention pinned on him.

Humans. Each one lovely, young and in heat. He could not help but smile, for he had only to pick one, unless they were open to sharing. Maka bless modern women.

He left his half-finished glass of Johnny Walker Blue on the bar and stalked toward his huntresses, closing the distance between himself and paradise. Music throbbed like a communal heartbeat and strobe lights flashed in weak imitation of the Thunderbirds' lightning.

All three straightened at his approach, standing in a cluster around a tall circular table that held their poser drinks, three martinis. It was hard to suppress his grin of anticipation.

The tallest and strongest had dark eyes and mocha skin. She had used black liner to accentuate her sloping eyes. The gold chain about her neck held a single black crystal bead that sparkled from its place in the cleft of her ample cleavage. This one wore a very short skirt, revealing long, strong legs that he anticipated wrapped about his back.

Beside her, stood a petite blonde who had teased her hair to add height. Her low-cut pink blouse showed her form to be sleek and athletic. She glanced from him to the tallest, as if seeking permission to advance. She licked her lips, perhaps admiring what she might not taste, as she struggled with her position as second to the tallest. She shifted her weight back and forth. Were she a wolf, he would anticipate a leadership challenge, but humans settled such battles more subtly. Perhaps *he* would be the one worth fighting for.

Flanking the alpha's opposite side was another brunette. Their eyes met. She was used to being overlooked, although she had the most interesting figure, with full, heavy breasts, a narrow waist and wide, curving hips. She glanced from him to the other women, already deferring her authority. As the group's beta, she would do as the others bid. That might work to his advantage.

He reached them now, smiling as he nodded his hello, keeping his eyes on the alpha female.

"Did you want to speak to me?"

Her sensual smile rewarded his direct approach.

"We have a bet on you."

"Interesting."

"You're what's interesting," said the blonde, her hand already on his shoulder, claiming him.

The alpha flashed her a look and the hand slid away. Not ready for a challenge just yet.

"We were wondering if you prefer blondes or brunettes. I'm Allie, by the way," said the alpha.

He pressed a hand to his chest and gave a little bow. "Nick. And I prefer both."

The beta's mouth rounded into an O, while the other two exchanged knowing looks that told him this was familiar territory.

"Do you?" asked Allie as she laid a hand on his shoulder, circling him. Her fingers dragged across his back and down his arm as she measured his strength. Nick watched the blonde, who did not take her eyes off her rival. Neither of the other women moved until Allie had linked her arm in his, claiming him. Only then did the emerging alpha move.

"I'm Krista," said the blonde, flanking him on the right and stroking his biceps.

The beta stayed where she was, caressing him only with her eyes.

"Would you ladies like a drink?"

"Love one. I have a full bar at my place," offered Allie as her long, artificial nails dug into his arm.

Nicholas flexed his muscles beneath her grip as a slow smile spread over his face. "Private party sounds good."

He was always up for such a diversion, especially in the winter, when the nights were long and lonely.

Allie signaled the waitress. Nick slid a single hundred-dollar bill from his money clip onto the waitress's tray.

Allie's eyes glittered in a way that made Nick wonder if perhaps these ladies were pros. Money was not an issue, but it did run counter to his loose moral code to pay for what he could find for free.

Allie smiled and slipped a hand into the gap at the collar of his black oxford shirt and unbuttoned the top one.

Great Mystery! Human females were a spirited lot. He thought of his friend Sebastian and all the lovely women his friend had never met, because he lived like a hermit in the woods. Sebastian was disapproving of Nick's philandering. So it irked Nick that his buddy had still somehow managed to find himself a life mate in Michaela Proud.

Nick fought the twinge of jealousy. Silly to begrudge Sebastian one woman when he had three willing partners before him. Still, Michaela was unique enough to make a confirmed bachelor envious. She had accepted his friend even after seeing him change from a man to a bear, and that did not happen every century. As if this were not gift enough, his friend described a connection, a reading of his mate's thoughts and emotions, something Nick had never experienced.

He imagined what would happen if he showed these females what he truly was. No, his way was best. Never let a human see you transform, never overstay your welcome. The rules served him well for there was no worse trap than giving your heart to a woman.

"Ready?" asked Allie, pursing her full lips.

Nick found her artful pout did not have the desired effect, for it irritated rather than inspired him. He disliked lipstick as well as the tangy aroma of foundation and powder. Most perfumes overwhelmed his sensitive sense of smell.

Now, for instance, he noted the acrid scent of the chemicals of her deodorant activated by her sweat, the mint mouthwash, the almond fragrance clinging to her hair, remnants of shampoo or rinse, a perfumed talcum powder and even the tanned leather of her purse. There was something wintergreen in her purse, likely gum or breath mints. Human females bathed themselves in every perfume but the most potent of all was the scent of their arousal. He sensed, in Allie, the first blossom of the lust she planned to share.

Her second reached the waitress and made sure Allie saw her slip the change into her bra. Her eyes set in a challenge directed at Allie, but the alpha chose to ignore her defiance, letting her keep the cash.

"Shall we?" said Alpha.

Nick helped her with her coat and then assisted her blonde second.

Beta hovered. If she had had a tail, it most certainly would have been tucked tightly between her legs.

Alpha paused and cast her a backward glance. "You coming, Becca?"

Becca hesitated, then followed the pack. Funny, she seemed physically the strongest, but that was not always what mattered in the battle for dominance.

They cleared the bar and stood on the sidewalk, still wet from the cold New York City rain. Nick's breath came in white puffs of condensing air. He wore no coat, nor did he need one. His leather jacket would keep him warm since it was, in fact, part of his own furry hide. Nick was of the wolf clan, and like his brothers, he could stand the bitter cold.

Even at this late hour, cabs lined up, hoping for a fare. Allie hailed one and then slid into the back, dragging him along. Krista tucked in beside him, leaving Beta the front seat with the cabbie.

"Second Avenue and Eighteenth," said Allie.

By the time they reached their destination, the woman had him half-undressed and hard as iron. He buttoned his trousers before exiting to follow the giggling women. The streetlights were switching off as night gave way to dawn but for him, the night was still young.

Allie paused to punch in a code on the entry box, releasing the heavy metal door. She turned, leaned against the panic bar and posed, giving him a come-hither stare. When he didn't move, she grabbed the lapel of his collar and dragged him along. They passed the rows of silver mailboxes.

Krista hit the elevator button. The doors of the waiting car creaked open and Beta stepped in first. Nick faced the panel of buttons.

released their hosts, causing all the women to fall to the pavement.

And he understood. They had not come to kill him—they had allowed him to escape. The ghosts did not want his mangy hide. They only used him to get to Sebastian, and to Michaela.

Nagi was hunting her again.

The Thunderbirds scooped him up, the beating of their mighty wings making the wind that lifted him and roared like a freight train. He shouted a warning, begging them to change their course, to bring him away from his friends. But the lightning cracked with earsplitting force and he feared they could not hear him.

Had the ghosts succeeded in joining the Whirlwind?

His head swam as he coughed up blood into the freezing air.

Still he cried his warning, growing dizzy from the pain. Nicholas struggled to remain conscious. He had to warn them. He had to tell Sebastian.

His vision blurred as he prayed he would not be the instrument that brought the Ruler of the Circle of Ghosts to his friends' doorstep.

Chapter 2

Jessie Healy saw the storm blowing down the valley toward her spread, a thunder dome so powerful it created twin twisters that reached sinuous black arms to the earth. The thunderstorm beat with a pulse of life and she recognized it from her mother's description. This was no ordinary gale, but a creation of the Thunderbirds. Her eyes narrowed as she watched the men scrambling to bring in the horses.

She stood beside the corral, gripping the sturdy pine post as the winds increased, trying to catch a glimpse of them, knowing that if she did so, she would be changed forever. And still she could not resist the chance to glimpse a true Spirit.

The flying debris finally forced a retreat. The farrier held open the barn door for her to enter. It took both him and his assistant to drag it shut behind them.

The howl of the wind reminded her of a freight train as it passed over them, shaking dust from the rafters and causing the old timbers to creak like the beams of a ship. Darkness descended in moments. The horses pawed the earth of their paddock, shifting nervously.

Jessie flicked on the lights, turning on the row of naked bulbs that lined the center of the barn. She did not try to speak over the shrieking wind. The roar diminished by degrees and the shower of hay settled as the twister passed.

"Lucky it didn't take off the roof," said Hal, the farrier, removing his hat and using his forearm to wipe the sweat from his brow. "Damned lucky."

He threw his rasp back into the open five-gallon bucket. The young man lifted the handle and headed toward the door, waiting for Hal to drag it back.

The tall grasses by the road now lay flat as if ironed, but beyond, her house remained standing. Hal's truck, sheltered beside the barn, had been polished clean of dust by the scouring rain.

She saw the black heap first and took a step in that direction. The object lay in the exact spot where she had been standing before taking cover. How odd.

Jessie continued forward, away from the men who were congratulating themselves over her rescue, which was ironic as it was her duty to protect them.

A leg became obvious first and then an arm.

"What's that?" asked Hal.

She saw him clearly now. He lay in a puddle of water, dressed in gray slacks, a black leather jacket and matching dress shirt. His clothing was soaking wet and his dark hair lay plastered to his head.

"It appears to be a man." Her eyes narrowed as she peered at him. His aura was wrong, very wrong.

"Holy hell," cried Hal.

He dashed forward and rolled the man to his back, revealing the deep gouges in his face, but Jessie focused on the aura.

"Looks like he was clawed by a wild cat," said the assistant. "Think it was that mountain lion?"

"You idiot. It was the storm," said Hal.

His assistant pointed. "How could a storm do that?"

"Right. Might more likely a cat attacked him and then the storm rescued him and dropped him here."

His assistant stopped arguing in favor of scratching his neck and staring down in puzzlement at the person in question.

The man's aura shone bright iridescent pink. That denoted sexual energy. The pale blue that encircled him like a bright bubble meant torture, and the black centered near his ribs, a brush with death.

Hal stooped with his ear just above the man's open mouth. "He's breathing."

Jessie saw the dark brown aura. Now that was a color she recognized instantly, for she had seen it before. This was no man.

"We gotta get him into the house," said Hal.

The barn would be more appropriate, she thought but could not reveal her revulsion without seeming a madwoman. He belonged in the woods, skulking about like the trickster he was. But she couldn't say so, for her people's law prohibited her from doing anything that would reveal who and what she truly was.

"Miss Healy?"

She glanced at the men to see them both staring at her with wary expressions. She did not want this enemy in her home.

"Yes, of course." She turned away, preceding them across the dirt road. Why would the Thunderbirds drop an Inanoka on her doorstep?

For reasons of their own, Thunderbirds protected these dreadful creatures and knew full well that their races hated each other. She had never even spoken to one but had seen them, one still in animal form and the other walking down the middle of the sidewalk of Billings, Montana, fooling the men, but not her.

Why, by the Great Spirit, would Thunder Spirits carry such treacherous creatures on their backs? No one had ever been able to answer that one to her satisfaction.

She had the door open and led the way to her study, situated beyond the kitchen and adjoining her bedroom. Choosing this room simply because she did not think the men could make it to the second floor. Across from the computer and overstuffed reading chair stood a daybed overflowing with pillows. She began piling them on the floor, finishing just as the men carried in the creature. They had one of its arms draped over each of their shoulders. His shoes dragged along between them, trailing dead leaves onto her clean floors.

They lowered him to the sunny yellow bedspread and all three stood over him.

"Look at those cuts," said the assistant.

"You might be right, Chuck. Something or somebody did that to him. I'd bet my bottom dollar on it." He turned his attention to her. "Real lucky for him he collapsed here, unless it wasn't luck. You think he was trying to reach you, Miss Healy?"

"How? I didn't see any car or truck," said his underling.

Let them try and work it out, she thought, knowing they never would. Creatures such as this had preyed on men for centuries. It was the responsibility of all Niyanoka to keep mankind safe from creatures like this, but to do so without them knowing of her people's benevolence.

Hal scratched his neck. "Damned strange. Better call the state police, I guess."

"Or the volunteer fire department. My brother-in-law is right up the road."

She felt a burst of relief, as if someone had turned on a warm, sweet shower to wash away all her troubles.

"Yes, let's do that." They could take him away. That would be best all around.

Hal leaned forward to examine the Skinwalker and Jessie tensed, ready to defend him if the creature showed any sign of aggression. She could not see much of his face past the bloody lacerations, but his dark hair was thick and straight, cut short on the sides, which— coupled with what she could see of his nose, mouth and jaw—confirmed he had blood of the first people. He had to if he was a Skinwalker.

"He's bringing up blood. Gonna need surgery, I'll bet."

Jessie went cold. Surgery meant anesthesia and that meant this damned thing would change back into a beast right there in front of a room full of doctors.

She couldn't let that happen. Jessie set her jaw against the bitter taste rising in her throat. She swallowed, knowing what she must do and feeling uncertain that she was up to the task. She had spent her entire adult life helping people and had never intentionally caused harm to any creature.

Even one like him.

Jessie fastened her gaze on the Skinwalker, pressed down by the weight of her responsibilities.

Her voice trembled only a little. "Phone is in the kitchen."

Hal stepped out, but the assistant remained.

She glanced at him, forcing herself not to fidget. "Get me a towel from the bathroom, Chuck."

As he turned to go, she nearly called him back but found her voice had deserted her. She adjusted her work gloves, pulling them over the cuffs of her long-sleeved shirt, before lifting a pillow from the floor, clutching it with trembling hands.

She had to. It was her duty to keep the humans from discovering about them and her purpose to protect humans from all threats, including shifters.

Her fingers sank into the soft foam and she hesitated. Her shoulders sagged. Then she held the pillow to her own face to stifle the sob. No matter what kind of monster he was, she could not kill him as he lay helpless before her. But she could not let him go to a hospital. What to do?

Something grabbed her wrist. The pillow dropped from her hand.

His crystal blue eyes glistened.

"Let go, shifter," she ordered, knowing he was the stronger.

His eyes narrowed as he yanked her forward, bringing her to her knees. She fell onto the area rug as he reeled her in, stopping only when their noses nearly touched.

He stared into her eyes for a moment, then snorted and released her wrist as if she posed little threat. She fell sideways onto the pillow that she had meant to use to smother him with just a moment before.

Bedtime stories of the cruel Inanoka rose in her mind. Why hadn't she killed him when she had the chance? She read the menace in his narrowing eyes, knowing with certainty she would never have succeeded. He was not as helpless as she assumed. His injuries served only to make him more dangerous, as lethal as any wounded animal. Even now, spitting blood, he was a threat.

The safest course was retreat. She scrambled out of his reach.

But she did not take her eye off him. When he did not attack, some of her indignation returned.

"What are you?" he snarled.

She lifted her chin. "Your better."

His smile was cold. "Such arrogance could come only from a Niyanoka."

She nodded. "Why are you here?"

"I don't know." He glanced about her room. "I asked the birds to take me to a healer."

"And they have done so. Is that *all* you asked?"

"No. To lead them away from my friends." His eyes fluttered and she saw them roll over white.

She straightened, preparing to flee, but he roused himself, mastering the momentary weakness. His eyes snapped open, locking on her.

Her heart hammered as she inched back.

"Lead who away?" she whispered, suddenly afraid of the answer.

"The ghosts. Nagi sent them to attack me so I would bring them to her."

The wolf must be deranged, because Nagi did not send ghosts to attack living creatures. He captured the evil ones after their death if they refused to walk the Way of Souls, forcing them to face judgment.

"Her? The healer you seek is also female?"

"Michaela. She's Niyanoka, like you. The last Seer of Souls and Nagi wants her dead."

She fell back to her seat on the carpet as the possibility of this ricocheted in her brain. Could it be true?

No—this was a Skinwalker. His currency was lies.

"Why should I believe you?" But she knew why. His black aura, the part that said he had been touched by death. Only a ghost could do that. But it made no sense.

Why would Nagi hunt one of her people and why would a Skinwalker want to protect her?

His intent blue eyes pinned her. She felt her mouth go

dry as she considered the impossible. Could the trickster be speaking the truth? Great Mystery, what evil was this?

She stared in astonishment and knew that to learn the answer, she would have to heal him herself.

Chapter 3

Nick glared up at the haughty face of the beautiful Niyanoka and wondered again why the Thunderbirds left him here.

He stared at her honey-brown eyes, lovely eyes—if they did not glare daggers at him. His gaze dipped to the full mouth and perfectly shaped upper lip, now stretched in a grimace as if he smelled of filth.

She had been trained from birth to hate Skinwalkers, to consider them a threat. He could hardly blame her, given their history—though there had been no attacks in nearly a century. But Niyanoka had long memories. Of a time when his people had banded together in an effort to take back the world from the humans who threatened the balance, and they had begun with their protectors.

It took everything he had to meet the accusation in her eyes without turning away. Shame flared fresh and sharp. His father had killed many of her kind and he felt the weight of responsibility at the blood he carried in his veins.

"My ribs are broken," he said, knowing he would gain no sympathy, for though they were both born of the union of human and Spirit, they were also born enemies. Yet the Thunderbeings had brought them together, placed him at the mercy of one without any.

He thought of what his father would have done had an injured Niyanoka fallen at his doorstep, and cringed.

She rose to her feet but came no closer. Her hands shook as she removed her gloves, but she clasped them before her quickly in an effort to hide her fear. She couldn't, of course, for he could smell it as clearly as he could smell the lanolin in the transparent gloss that coated her lips.

"If they take you to the hospital, they'll see what you are."

"So you decided to smother me." The words cost him greatly, but he would not let her see any physical weakness. He kept his jaw locked against the grinding pain of each breath.

"A poor attempt. I've spent too much time nurturing creatures. It seems I can't even kill the dangerous ones."

So she counted him no more than a stray dog. His mouth twisted in a humorless smile.

She glanced over her shoulder. "You can't let them take you."

"You think I would do better in your tender hands?" He managed to lift one eyebrow and found that even that hurt. The possessed females had mangled his face with their acrylic claws. He was surprised to see her face flush, almost as if she regretted her actions. Could she have a conscience, after all?

"We have a duty to our races. Your identity must remain secret."

"How?"

"Is there someone you can call, some family member or friend?"

Nick glanced away. He had employees, scores of them, all over the country, working on various projects to reclaim land into the wild, funded primarily by his investment company, Wolf Investments, which was a lucrative collection of managed sustainable funds traded on the S&P 500. But he had no family or clan or mate. He purposely lived a solitary life by design to keep himself from dangerous entanglements. Up until a few hours ago, he had never needed help from anyone. But all that had changed.

"There must be someone." Her voice held incredulity, as if it was impossible to find him so alone in the world. He staunched the pain that was a familiar companion. It was better than the alternative. He glared up at her.

She understood now. He saw it in the astonishment rounding her eyes. Still it took another moment for her to fathom. His way was so different than the way of her people, who lived in small tight communities.

"Where are your people?" she whispered.

"I have none."

She nodded, as thoughtful as a priest hearing confession. "All right, then. No one can force you to go to the hospital. Refuse treatment and I'll agree to keep you here."

"I'd do better lying by the roadside."

She glanced toward the door, hearing the approaching footsteps, at last.

"They're coming. I swear I'll do my best to keep you alive *if* you agree to stay here."

He did not trust her, but he did trust the Thunderbirds. They had left him here for a reason. And even though he did not understand their purpose, he accepted it.

"Yes," he said, cradling his fractured ribs. Damned if he'd let her see his agony. The world swam, and next thing he knew, two young men knelt beside him. One looked like a young Abe Lincoln, all sharp angles and homely hollows, while the other had oily, blemished skin that said he loved fried food better than a long life.

"Relax, sir. We're going to take you to the hospital."

"No," he said.

Fast Food leaned in, his breath smelling of onions. "Listen, buddy, your face looks like raw hamburger. Might get infected, plus the doc says you broke some ribs."

He glanced at his reluctant benefactor. Was she the doctor they spoke of? He kept his gaze pinned to her and said, "I refuse to go to a hospital."

She smiled her approval and his breath caught at the radiance of her beauty. The intake of breath cost him, sending him into coughing fits that brought up bubbly pink blood.

"He's got internal bleeding," said Fry Boy.

"It's his choice," said the Niyanoka.

"Who's going to take care of him?"

"I am," she said.

The men turned to her. "He's busted up, Doc. Not loopy."

"All psychiatrists are also medical doctors. Besides, he might be better here than bouncing over ninety miles of rough road."

The men exchanged looks.

Young Abe held out a clipboard to Nick. "Sign here."

The woman looked concerned. Did she think he could not write? Nick lifted the pen and carefully scrawled his name, making certain the grace of his signature was clear. He glanced at her and saw her shoulders droop in relief.

What had they taught her about his kind?

She hustled out the medics. The two men who had carried him into the house followed them out. She closed the door firmly behind her without even glancing back at him. He let his head drop back to the pillow and closed his eyes, taking shallow breaths as blood dripped from the gashes on his face and into the soft clean coverlet. he wondered if he had just made the worst mistake of his life.

No. The worst mistake was getting in that elevator with three ghosts.

The room smelled of lemon polish and wax. The bedding held a hint of bleach and detergent. Across the room a bowl of wood shavings released the scent of cedar into the air.

Dr. Niyanoka's life was about to get real messy.

The click of the doorknob awakened him and he opened one swollen eye to watch her approach carrying a medical bag and a basin. The smell of soap and disinfectant rose from the warm water.

He lay still when she drew up the chair beside him and set the bowl on the bedside table. She rummaged through her bag, drawing out two rubber gloves. How humiliating it must be for her to have to touch him.

She uncapped a needle and plunged the tip into a vial and faced him with weapon raised. He prepared to fight and she drew to a halt.

"It's medicine, for the pain," she said.

"So was the pillow."

She held out the vial, then changed her mind and read the label to him. He took it and forced his good eye open enough to read the contents. Would she have switched the contents? He stared up at her. Her expression was strained, but her body held none of the hesitation or uncertainty she radiated earlier. He trusted his instincts and lay back on the bed. A moment later she had his hip exposed and swabbed. The prick was nothing compared to the stabbing of each breath.

The drug burned into his muscle and his ears began to ring. His body grew heavy. Thoughts grew difficult to gather as the drug traveled through his system, but he breathed without pain for the first time since the attack.

He grinned at her tight expression and felt an echoing twitch of pain, dulled by the medication. She looked grim as she wrung out the dish towel and then gripped it firmly in her clenched fist. She hesitated, the cloth hovering above him.

"I won't bite," he assured.

She sighed and then washed the blood from his face. Her gentleness surprised him. He knew the task could be accomplished with a much more punishing stroke, but she seemed to strive not to cause him additional pain, though she avoided touching him as well, as she plied the cloth with the gloved hand.

"What's your name?" he asked.

"Jessie Healy. Yours?"

"Nicholas Chien. Where am I?"

"Freehold, Montana, two hundred miles west of Billings."

His eyelids grew heavy, but he fought off the lethargy.

"You're a sight," she murmured.

For the first time he thought to wonder what he really looked like. For years he'd relied on his good looks to get him exactly what he wanted from women, and he realized with a nasty lurch that he had lost one major advantage. Those women had gouged his face as if it were warm wax. He allowed himself to relax as she bathed his face and neck.

"Are you certain they were ghosts?"

He didn't open his eyes. "Positive."

"How do you know?"

"The stink. They smell like death and their eyes take on an unnatural yellow glow."

The drug made him woozy but did its work. He

made an investigatory pat of his face as she drew out a stethoscope and listened to his chest.

"Your lung is collapsed. We need to get you looked at."

His friend Sebastian would have him whole already. "I thought you were a healer."

"I am, but I can't reinflate your lung. It wouldn't be safe. I have a friend. He can do surgery on-site. He's very good."

His thoughts were harder to gather. He tried to focus on why this was a bad idea. It came to him at last as he recalled her earlier concern that he may go wolf on the operating table. "Anesthesia?"

"It won't matter."

He opened his eyes and their gazes met. Her face flushed and he knew she was up to something.

She tried for a smile of reassurance, but it flickered and died before reaching her golden eyes.

"He's a large-animal vet."

Nick drew a breath to protest but choked on the blood in his throat and managed only a gurgle.

"Now listen, if he puts you out, you'll already be in animal form."

Nick groaned again. "What if he puts me down instead of out?"

"I won't let that happen."

This from a woman who had already tried to smother him.

"Why don't I feel better?" he muttered.

"I promise to do everything I can to help you. You have to trust me."

Trust a woman. That was funny. He'd laugh if his rib wasn't jabbing his lung. Instead, he tried to think of another way. He had never been to a vet. The very thought was humiliating, but he had a nasty suspicion that he'd die otherwise. Given the people he needed to protect, he couldn't do that.

Nick nodded his acceptance.

"I have to get you into the truck," she said. "I think, if you change, I can carry you."

He looked at her and knew she couldn't do it. He sat up. Even with the painkillers chugging through his system, the effort covered him in a cold sweat. Together they made it to the front steps. He was dribbling frothy pink blood from his mouth again and coughing. Pinpricks of light spun about him as he gripped the railing.

"I'll get the truck."

She set off at a run, bounding like a deer, and he wished he had the strength to give chase. The truck roared up to the steps. He lifted his head from the crook of his arm, not even recalling assuming that position.

She wrapped an arm around his broken rib cage. The pain nearly buckled his knees.

He made it to the door and staggered into the truck. She rounded the hood and jumped into the driver's side. She reached for the clutch then hesitated, leaving them in place.

"I'll have help at the vets. Maybe you should change now." She gripped the steering wheel as if bracing for a blow.

Nick studied her. "You gave your word."

He waited until she nodded her acceptance before focusing his dwindling energy on the change. The power zinged through his veins, momentarily overcoming the pain. Then he coiled into the position of a wounded animal upon her vinyl seat.

He kept his gaze on her as she stared in wide-eyed astonishment.

"A wolf," she whispered and he realized that she had not known his animal form when she agreed to tend him. Did it make a difference? It was certain it would to some. Had she been there—during the war?

Her face paled as her bloodless fingers slipped from the wheel. She threw open the door and slid from the truck, pausing only to slam the door in his face. She kept both hands on the metal exterior as she stared in horror through the closed window.

So much for the truce they had forged. It seemed that Skinwalkers were not the only ones who could not be trusted.

Nick woke in the arms of a barrel-chested man whose booming baritone voice ordered someone to hold the door.

"Jessie, I don't care what your friend said. This here's a damned wolf."

"He's gentle, I swear," she said, vouching for his character.

"Folk round don't patch wolves. They shoot 'em."

"Well, I want him patched."

"Car hit him?"

Nick was swung through the door and carried past

rows of plastic chairs. The scent of cat, urine, dog and ferret all assaulted him in a nauseating wave of odor and he did not hear her answer.

She hadn't abandoned him, then. What had changed her mind?

"What happened to his face?"

"I don't know. But his ribs are broken."

"Tangled with a bear, maybe. Sure you don't want to just put him out of his misery?"

Was it the real purpose of this visit? Nick started to struggle but the man simply tightened his stranglehold. Nick's injuries made him weak, too weak to transform again.

Behind him, Jessie Healy's voice rang with adamancy. "Absolutely not!"

"Might be expensive."

"Just do it."

Nick liked the sharp ring of authority in her tone. They laid him on his side on a cold metal table that stank of disinfectant and fear. The vet had his back to him for a moment. When he turned, he held a huge needle.

Nick scrambled, but the vet grasped the scruff of his neck.

"Hold him, Jess."

She laid trembling hands on his hip and he stilled instantly, feeling the assault of stubborn resolve that was not his own. Was he crazy? She was Niyanoka and his interests were not the same as hers. She had given her word, but she had given it to a creature who she considered to be her inferior and her enemy. Panic rushed like fire through his veins and he tried to rise to his feet.

Nick felt the pinch as the needle punctured his scruff. There was a burning and then his legs went out from under him.

Chapter 4

Nagi was still in possession of the young man's body when the ghosts arrived, all three of them, pulsing weakly and stinking of failure. Rage ripped through him as the excuses began. They had located him in the living world, where he came to collect errant ghosts for his circle. But tonight he was attending to a very personal matter which they were interrupting.

He led them outdoors to the cool, familiar darkness of the night and did not stop until he was well away from the house. There, beneath the shimmering canopy of silver stars, he paused to face them.

"My lord and master," said the first, "we did as you bid and attacked the Tracker and—"

The arsonist interrupted, "But we did not kill him, as you commanded."

The third said nothing.

The first continued as if the others were not there. "And we allowed him to escape before following."

"Then why are you here, groveling like sick dogs?"

The arsonist became more transparent. "He did not go to the Healer."

"What!" Nagi extended his human arms, sending a shock wave forward with such force it threw all three ghosts back into a series of somersaults. The only thing that kept him from casting them to the very bottom of his circle was the need for more answers.

"Where is he?" Nagi shouted.

The first ghost's voice faltered. "H-he found a Dream Walker."

Nagi glared. Why would an Inanoka travel to an enemy when a friend could heal him? He fixed his gaze on the center ghost, the one who thought killing his wife would keep her from loving another. Why did he not speak?

And then he understood. Holding the fury at bay, he spoke to the third specter.

The icy calm brought the vibrating forms before him to stillness. "You warned him, didn't you?"

"We didn't, my lord," said the first, then glanced at his comrades and in that instant chose his soul over theirs. He pointed at the silent one. "He did. While still in the woman's body, he called to us that the Inanoka was taking us to the Seer. The Tracker must have heard him."

"So he changed course."

No one spoke.

"And why does it require three of you to bring me this message?"

No answer.

"Who guards the Inanoka in your absence?"

Animosity pulsed bright red between the three and he knew all. None trusted the others out of their sight, so they had abandoned their posts to come to him.

"All of you were called to the Spirit Road at your death. But you did not come. When I captured you, I gave you what none before you had ever received—a chance. This is how I am repaid. I am keeper of the souls of the unwanted. But you—" he pointed at the culprit "—are unwanted even by me."

A jade spark issued from his hand. The killing orb shot at the third ghost, igniting his soul until he blazed bright as green lightning.

Nagi was disgusted by his own choices. He should have taken more time to pick his soldiers instead of enlisting the first three sorry ghosts he captured.

He turned his attention on the two remaining souls.

"Tell me where he is." They did, but he was not satisfied.

"You left your post. What shall I do with two deserters?" He lifted his human hand to the stars, opening a portal. There the Ghost Road glittered, leading the way to the Spirit World, a world they would never see.

"You will now walk the path you are destined to tread."

Nagi waited. The ghosts both looked relieved. He had not extinguished their souls. But in time, they would wish he had.

He allowed them only one step upon the Way of Souls. Hihankara, the crone that guarded the road, appeared before them instantly, her grim continence relaying that these two would never pass.

He called to them and they turned.

"Both of you have living family." He looked at the first. "You a mother." And then to the arsonist. "You a sister. Both live worthy lives. I count their prayers. In time, you might have been released from my circle. But for your failings, I condemn you to the bottom level of my circle, from which none escape."

Nagi lifted his hand.

"My lord, wait."

He exhaled and his breath swept them from the road. He watched them tumble through space, screaming and clawing as they dropped through the center of his spinning circle of souls, through the ghosts who might someday reach the Spirit World, past those without hope, into the circle of despair. Here the ghosts did not walk in an endless circle. Here they stood, packed as close as cattle in a slaughterhouse. But the closeness did not warm them. In icy silence they called, unable to move, unable to see or hear even their own voices. There were worse things than death, far, far worse.

Satisfied, he strode across the lawn, wishing he could feel the dew that clung to this body's bare feet. But his human host was only a puppet at his command. He could not feel or taste. In fact, he could not recall if he had allowed this body to eat since he took him. He decided to stop in the kitchen for some nourishment. It would not do to have his host expire before he was done with him.

Chapter 5

It was midafternoon before Jessie arrived home with the wolf, still seething over their agreement. He had proved her suspicion correct by his lie of omission. A wolf!

The vet had wanted to put him down and, Maka help her, she had been tempted. Then he asked to keep Nick overnight, but she did not dare leave him for fear he'd come to and transform. After trying and failing to lift Nick from her truck, she'd been forced to call for help, but not to her parents. Great Mystery, no!

There was nothing her people hated more than a wolf. The very reason her people no longer lived in large groups was because of a great gray timber wolf. His name was Fleetfoot and he led the uprising. His army of Skinwalkers nearly destroyed them. His death marked the turning point. After the Niyanoka victory, they broke into small bands, hiding among the humans they protected. Since the Skinwalkers could not see auras, they could not differentiate between men and Spirit Child. Their invisibility acted as a defense tactic, a sort of camouflage, should the truce between their people ever be broken. Thus far, the agreement remained intact. But for those who lived through the bloodshed, the war would never end. Her people had vowed that the Skinwalkers would never again find them amassed in one place. From that day to this, they lived among humans, hiding in plain sight.

Jessie did not like asking for help, but in the end she called her neighbor, up the road. While she waited, her mind filled with images of terrible stories her mother had told her after surviving the war between the races. Her mom had witnessed the bloodshed caused by Inanoka.

Why hadn't Nick told her his animal form was wolf?

But she knew. He tricked her. Somehow he had known that if she even suspected he was a wolf, she would never have entered into that cursed bargain.

Larry Karr pulled in, a little too eager to help. But he groaned when he lifted Nick, succeeding in extracting him from the truck.

"He's heavier than you'd think," he said, a sheen of sweat breaking out on his pink face.

Larry carried the sedated wolf into the house with Jessie leading the way to her guest room off the kitchen.

"Put him on the bed," she said.

Larry, out of breath now and puffing like a power

lifter, hesitated only a moment before doing as she requested. Once unburdened, he gazed down at the large gray timber wolf with a solemn expression. "You sure that thing is tame?"

Jessie wasn't—for she could think of nothing more wild or unpredictable than a wolf.

Her silence seemed to reinforce Larry's concerns. The rancher had a spread just south of her place and had likely shot a few wolves, regardless of the laws. He shifted his watery eyes from the canine to her.

"Maybe I best put him in the barn. You got a cage out there?"

She did, the one she used to house her Labrador pup. But that was years ago. Her mother had hated the dog, hated all animals that reminded her of wolves and bears.

Jessie reviewed her promise and wondered if she had said anything that prevented her from caging this Skinwalker. Fear of him warred with her obligation to do her best to care for him.

"Better leave him there."

"Might roll off. Might bite you. Hate you to have to get rabies shots over some mangy sheep killer."

Nick was anything but mangy. His coat would be the envy of any woman who ever dressed in fur. Why had she promised to care for him?

She turned to Larry. She had lived only ten years in this place and she could safely stay another fifteen before people began to notice that she did not age like the rest of them, for her life expectancy could be up to four hundred years. She liked it here, but recognized that this problem might expose her. Her neighbor could not know about Halflings. Niyanoka law forbade revealing who and what they were.

"He won't bite me. I told you. He's a pet." She took a tentative step forward and rested trembling fingers on Nick's head, hoping he didn't awaken and take off her hand. The instant her fingers slipped into the thick, soft coat, she sensed the tingling sensation of power. The texture was as sensual as anything she had ever touched. Even sedated, Nick radiated strength and energy. She found herself stroking him from his ear to the thick scruff at his neck. It was a coat to burrow into, with lush outer hair and soft, thick inner fur that protected him.

But it was a coat he could shed at will and slip into the midst of humans, tricking them into believing he was something he was not—just as he had done to her. Jessie fumed. He was a born deceiver and dangerous, yes, far more dangerous than Larry could ever imagine.

Jessie gazed down at the white bandage on the wolf's side. Three of his ribs were broken, as if he'd been kicked by an elk. But that didn't explain the gouges. One of his eyes was patched, but the claw marks on his muzzle were not. The vet had chosen to stitch them and leave them uncovered to heal. He had not been careful with the stitches, and Jessie felt a little sick with worry about what the Skinwalker would say when he found his face so roughly patched. Had he been in human form, such injuries would have warranted a plastic surgeon or at the very least a smaller gauge needle and thread.

"That damned thing might have one of my lambs in his belly right now."

Time for Larry to go. She turned to him and smiled, knowing she should offer him coffee. But Larry was married and seemed a little too interested in helping her out today.

"Thanks so much. I can take it from here." Jessie put a hand on Larry's shoulder, trying to usher him from the room. He took the hint and headed out through the kitchen, but paused on the front step.

"Sure I can't…"

"Thanks again. Appreciate your help."

He didn't move.

"Give my love to May and your girls."

That was the push he needed. He ambled back to his pickup and gave a wave from the open window before pulling onto the road and out of sight.

Jessie watched the rooster tail of dust in his wake and breathed a sigh of relief. It was a good five seconds before the disquiet returned, prickling up her spine like a rolling cactus. She had a wolf in her house.

If her mother found out, she'd kill him, her—or both.

She made her way back to her patient, studying his limp form. There was a small bandage covering the spot where the vet had shaved his coat to insert a tube that reinflated his lung. All in all he looked much worse than when she had taken charge of him. It would have been easy to let the vet put him down. Her mother would have approved.

Was a promise still a promise when given to the enemy?

Jessie sat beside him on the bed. She didn't know

when she began to stroke his long, muscular side, but at some point she noticed her hand half buried in fur as it made a rhythmic sweep. His steady breathing and the slow rhythmic beat of his heart reassured her.

"You're so soft."

It was past time to feed the horses, but she stayed where she was, as guardian or keeper, she was not sure which.

He gave a growl and his legs startled as if in the midst of a falling dream. She jumped back and succeeded in scrambling off the bed before Nick's uncovered eye snapped open.

The black pupil contracted as he cut his husky-blue eye in her direction.

"Why the hell didn't you tell me you were a wolf?" she asked, her fury boiling into her words.

Nick could not answer in animal form. But he narrowed his unpatched eye.

She leveled a gaze upon him. "Did you fight, Nick?"

He met her gaze and held it, lifting his muzzle in a defiant posture, and then shook his head.

"Your clan, then."

He didn't deny it. He was kin to all wolf shifters, including the most notorious.

Nick glared at her, his body aching all over. For some reason she had not killed him. But she had chosen not to cover him and that meant he would transform wearing nothing but his wolf pelt as a cloak. Then he need only touch his cloak to change it into any garment he desired. But he was not sure he could lift his arm. He tried his legs and discovered that they did not respond to his preliminary command, either. Had they paralyzed him?

Nick closed his eyes and concentrated, feeling the rush of electrical energy that always came when he changed. For an instant it overwhelmed the pain. The bandage over his eye tore away as his face changed shape. He bit down to keep from screaming as the pain flooded into the energy vacuum.

How he missed his friend Sebastian. The grizzly could fix him up in a matter of minutes. But he did not know if the ghosts had succeeded in following him and he would not take the risk of endangering his friend. That meant he was left with traditional Western medicine and that meant drugs.

Jessie was on her feet now, staring wide-eyed at him. You'd think she'd never seen a wolf transform into a man. He tried to smile and failed, managing only to bare his teeth.

She dragged a maroon-colored knit blanket from the back of her chair and tossed it over him as if casting a fishnet for minnows. Her efforts succeeded in covering his privates.

"Did you know him?" she asked and held her breath waiting for the answer.

"Who?"

"Fleetfoot."

"Very well."

She wrapped her arms about herself. "How?"

Cold blue eyes stared at her. "Fleetfoot was my sire."

She was on her feet in an instant and fleeing the room. She didn't stop until she was in the living room, standing before the loaded gun in the gun safe.

Fleetfoot's son. She started to shake.

"Jessie!"

She flinched at the power of his voice.

"Jessie, come back."

She did, but when she came, she carried with her a 32-caliber automatic rifle.

Chapter 6

What had possessed Nick to tell her the truth?

He must have landed on his head. He'd spent his entire adult life denying his paternity, roaming from place to place trying to forget what he was.

So why tell his secret to *her* when he had shared it with no one else? Her people had been the victims of his father's bloodletting. Skinwalkers were nothing if not effective killers. All his education and attempts at refinement were stripped away by this woman's hatred. She saw beneath the mask of civility to the beast within.

How would he feel if their roles were reversed?

He heard her coming. Nick managed to get one finger on the edge of his cloak, transforming his hide into a pair of jeans and the wolf-claw necklace he always wore when in human form. But the effort cost him, bringing a sheen of sweat to his skin.

He crawled off the bed and limped toward the door when the crazy Niyanoka returned with a rifle leveled at his gut. She'd moved up from the pillow. Now at least, she had a chance of taking him out, slim though it was.

While it was true that Skinwalkers were immune to most diseases and had a life expectancy some four times that of humans, they could not outrun a bullet. Injury, not illness, took out most Inanoka. His father had died of gunshot wounds and now he seemed about to follow in his sire's infamous tracks.

"You promised to take care of me."

"And I'm about to." She lifted the rifle.

The effort of getting off the bed and onto his feet had taken much of his strength. Still, even in his injured state, he had more than enough power to disarm her, before she ever pulled that trigger. But he did not, could not, harm her, even as she aimed the gun at his heart. What was wrong with him?

"I'm not my father," he said.

"You're his line. Fleetfoot killed my grandparents, my uncles, everyone but my mom." She pressed her face against the stock and braced, her feet wide apart, in preparation for the kill shot. And still he waited, motionless.

Had the Thunderbirds brought him here to meet his death? He stood silent and still before this woman who knew his shame.

If she had the nerve, he would take the bullet standing

like a man. There was no helping that he would change back to an animal at his passing.

"I could say you attacked me," she whispered, more to herself than to him. "They all said I was crazy not to put you down."

He said nothing in his own defense.

And then it came to him, the understanding he sought. If he died, Sebastian would be safe. The ghosts could not use him once he passed from their reach. Was this what the Thunderbirds intended when he begged them to protect his friend?

She held her position until beads of sweat formed on her forehead. Her indecision was palpable.

She gripped the barrel and released the stock. The gun swung upright. "God damn it!"

She wrapped both hands around the steel, as if trying to choke it to death.

Twice now she had failed to kill him.

"Get back in bed," she ordered.

She stayed where she was, watching him return to the sanctuary of his bed...*her* bed.

"You going to stare me to death?" he asked.

"If only." She turned to go and then spun to face him again. "Not only am I harboring an enemy. I'm harboring a descendant of the creature who tried to exterminate my people. Give me one reason why I shouldn't kill you."

"Because you don't seem capable of it."

She flushed. "You're a killer."

"My father was the killer. Would you judge a man whose father was in Hitler's SS?"

"Interesting comparison, since your father decided to kill men and Niyanoka alike."

"To protect the sacred buffalo when mankind was exterminating them for sport. He acted only when your people failed to take action to restore the balance."

She cocked the rifle but did not take aim. "You're one of them!"

"I was too young to choose a side."

"But it's in your blood. At heart, you are an animal."

"As are all men."

She scowled. "You are a smooth talker, just like a trickster. But how can I believe anything you say?"

He did not like to have his integrity questioned, but if anyone had the right, it was this woman.

She held the rifle before her as she spoke. "That story about the Niyanoka marrying a Skinwalker. Admit it, you made the whole thing up to play on my sympathy. The ghosts, Nagi, all of it."

He didn't succeed in curbing his anger at this. "That damn cloud of vapor nearly killed Michaela, attacking her using the dead body of her stepfather."

"Ha!" she said and pointed, as if catching him. "Ghosts can't possess the dead."

Nick lowered his chin and glared. "Nagi is not a ghost."

She lowered her arm, looking momentarily chastened, and uncocked the trigger of the rifle. "How did she escape him?"

"My friend Sebastian attacked him. He is a grizzly shifter, very strong and a great healer. He found Michaela after Nagi's first attack. She had a Spirit Wound."

Jessie paled and sank into her usual chair, laying the rifle across her knees. Clearly she was familiar with the kind of harm a true spirit could do to the soul, while leaving the body seemingly intact. Madness, coma, an unexplained wasting away could all be the result of such injury.

"My friend saved her life." He left the implication unsaid. A Skinwalker had saved a Spirit Child. It was her turn to return the favor.

"But how could he heal a Spirit Wound?" She leaned forward now, forgetting her skepticism.

"He couldn't, though he tried. All his efforts only succeeded in keeping her alive. So he brought her to Kanka."

Jessie's hands came up to cover her face. "He *met* the Witch?"

"He indebted himself to her."

"Great Mystery," she muttered.

"Exactly. Nagi was tracking Michaela using the Spirit Wound. Kanka gave Michaela the knowledge she needed to heal the wound. Nagi still wants her, but he can no longer track her. My friend has taken her into hiding until after her pregnancy."

Jessie could not contain her shock. "She's…"

He nodded. "With twins."

"But what, what will…"

He gave a sad smile. "Whatever they are, my friend will defend them with his life. He's not fast, but he's powerful as any creature I've ever faced. And I have no doubt that Michaela will be as fierce a mother as any Skinwalker and will love them unconditionally. *She* does not judge by appearances."

Jessie considered that in silence a moment.

"But how could she marry him?"

"She was raised by humans. Never knew who and what she was until after Nagi attacked her."

"Well, what difference does that make?"

He shook his head and then leveled his gaze on her once more. "She had no knowledge of your laws, your beliefs or your prejudices."

Jessie's indignation brought her to her feet. "More likely she does not know how treacherous Skinwalkers can be. She does not know how your people attacked mine or why we no longer dare live in clans. It is not so easy for you to find us now. Is it?"

"If what you say is true, then why did Sebastian not kill Michaela the instant he found her?"

"How do I know he did not? How do I know these two lovers even exist?"

He had no answer. A moment later he closed his eyes and then opened them to pin her with a look. She had not seen this expression before and it terrified her. He stared with the cold dispassion of a hunter.

"Then why have I not killed you?" he asked, his voice flat and devoid of emotion.

She stood, gripping the rifle. "Because I've given you no opportunity."

He laughed. An instant later he was across the room, seizing the rifle with one hand as he tore it from her and tossed it to the bed. He towered over her. She backed up, hit the chair and fell into the cushions. He gripped the armrests as he leaned over her and whispered in her ear.

"I have not killed you for two reasons. We have an agreement and I do not kill your kind."

He stood, stepping back far enough for her to rise. She found her knees trembling as she gained her feet. All this time she had thought him helpless and he was anything but.

"How could you move like that? Your injuries, your lungs."

"I am far stronger than a man."

He had made his point. He could have killed her anytime but didn't.

She stared up at him, trying to understand. It was then that she noticed the pallor of his skin. He had just had surgery and should be resting. Guilt stabbed her.

"How much pain?" she asked.

He gave her a weak smile. "I've had worse."

"I'll get your medicine."

She retrieved her rifle. Once out of his room, she unloaded the gun and replaced it in the case.

Only then did the trembling consume her. He could have killed her but didn't. Was he her enemy? Did he tell the truth? She'd never been more confused in her life.

She needed to know what was true. Was there a Seer of Souls? Was it possible that a Spirit Child would wed a Skinwalker and carry his children?

She glanced toward her patient's room. There was one way to find her answers. But she had never even met a Skinwalker before and so she did not even know if they dreamed.

But if he dreamed, she would have her chance to learn the truth.

She returned carrying the narrow white paper bag, and began removing orange canisters of medication.

"Decided to put off killing me?"

She smiled. "For now."

"Because I'm stronger than you or because of your promise?"

"Both."

He glanced at the bottle she gave him. "What is this?"

She inched closer. "Would you like me to read it to you?"

He furrowed his brow as a suspicion clouded his mind. "I can read."

Her astonished expression revealed her prejudice. "You can?"

"In six human languages."

Jessie's jaw dropped in shock.

He glanced at the ingredients of the narcotic and then removed two capsules.

"I'm supposed to hide it in raw hamburger," she said.

He glanced up in surprise. Her face gave nothing away and he could not quite tell if she was teasing him or serious.

"I shouldn't think that would be necessary." He popped the pills, chewing them to dust.

She wrinkled her face. "Isn't it bitter?"

"I've tasted worse."

She resumed her place on the far side of the room. "Do you think, I mean, could you…" She pointed at him. "Put on something more formal?"

He stared at his bare chest, hoping his undress unsettled her in a good way. He lifted a hand and touched his necklace, transforming his jeans into a full tuxedo with bow tie, undone.

"Better?"

Her initial shock gave way to a narrowing of her eyes, which she couldn't maintain, and she laughed aloud. The musical tinkling was charming and encouraging. He touched his necklace a second time and his attire morphed again. Now he lay in loose-fitting denim carpenter's pants and a sage-colored button-up shirt that would allow easy access to his wounds. He noticed a square three-inch hole in the fabric and lifted the shirt to examine the gap.

"They shaved me," he muttered.

"For the chest tube. Lots of blood in your lung."

It explained why he felt so weak, but already his body was healing at an accelerated rate.

She inched closer. "How do you do that?"

"We are half man. This state is as natural as our animal form."

"I meant the clothing. It seems like magic."

He hesitated, deliberating before answering. It was not wise to provide her with information she could use against him, but to answer her might help bridge the gap between them. Something in her eyes called to him and so he told her the truth.

"When in human form, we retain our coat. It allows us to transform back."

"But you don't have your coat now."

He lifted his shirt collar. "I do. It can take any form,

cloth, metal, bone, gemstone, as long as we wear it, to keep it safe."

Her eyes widened in comprehension. "Your necklace."

He nodded. "Many Inanoka wear their coat as a necklace, but I know a dolphin in Seattle who likes a tongue ring. It prevents her from losing her jewelry in the ocean."

"Dolphin? I had no idea."

It seemed to Nick she had no idea on many counts, but he kept his opinion to himself.

"What about you? What is your gift?"

Now it was her turn to hesitate. He waited patiently for her answer.

"I'm a Dream Walker."

"I've heard of you. You can heal wounds while a person sleeps."

"My uncle has that gift, to heal physical wounds. I heal psychic wounds. I'm a social worker, working mainly with child services. That allows me to explore what a patient is unwilling or unable to verbalize."

"By sneaking into their dreams?"

"I'm a professional. But essentially, that's right. They never remember our conversations or the events they reveal to me, so my intrusion is very minimal. But while I am there, I can heal trauma, plant ideas, offer strategies and unearth truths that would take years to discover by conventional means. I can also learn if a crime is being committed. I work with the police when I find child abuse."

"You protect those least able to protect themselves."

It was a noble endeavor, but he wondered if it might be very depressing at times.

The medicine had already taken the edge off the pain, making it easier to breathe but harder to concentrate.

"Do you think you can rest now?" she asked.

He nodded.

Something in her smile put him on guard. She wouldn't attack him when he slept, would she?

She retrieved the blanket and draped it over him before drawing back. "When you wake up, I can give you something to eat. What kind of things do you normally, uh, prefer?"

The tension in her posture and her uneasy expression nearly made him laugh. Likely she expected him to hamstring and eviscerate one of her horses.

"Roadkill is good. I don't have to kill it myself."

Horror blossomed on her face as she inched back.

He grinned, pulling at his stitches.

She cocked her head to study him. "Are you teasing me?"

"Yes," he said. "Were you kidding me about the raw hamburger?"

She chuckled. "Yes."

He was rewarded with her smile.

She turned toward the door, pausing at the entrance. "I think I saw a flattened ground squirrel out there. I could scrape it off the highway for you." He liked her playful expression and impish smile.

He made a face.

"What do you really eat?"

He realized she was now serious. She had no idea

what to prepare. "Generally, in human form, I eat what you eat, though I don't much like vegetables. Mostly grains and red meat, fish and poultry. When I was in Paris, I grew fond of wine sauces but never could get used to escargot."

"Paris?" Jessie couldn't even verbalize her shock. She had assumed this wolf lived in the forests, taking down sick elk or moose trapped in deep snow. The idea that he had been to Europe, spoke six languages and could read was all blowing her mind.

"You don't think much of us, do you?" he asked.

"I just…" Just what, have been misinformed her entire life? Everything she'd learned about Inanoka was tossed on its ear by this lone wolf.

Since she'd been old enough to understand, she had heard about his kind. About the tricksters who had nearly annihilated her race. Brutish, illiterate savages, killers with a dangerous propensity toward unpredictability and viciousness.

Now she stood beside a man who seemed to have tastes more refined than her own, and he'd showed amazing restraint when she threatened him. He could easily have killed her but didn't.

She bit her lip before asking the question, fearing his answer already. "What do you read?"

"I like nonfiction. For a time I read everything I could on ancient Rome. But lately I'm interested in the Middle East and North Africa. Fascinating people there, such dichotomy, but the culture is ancient. I'd like to go there next. Trying to learn Arabic. The written language is a challenge, but…" He smiled. "I've grown another head, haven't I?"

The magnitude of her prejudice was only now becoming evident. "I've, it's just… You are not what I expected."

"Likewise, except for the pillow. That's more in line with what I'm used to."

She felt a moment's shame.

"Are you hungry?" she asked.

His gaze flicked to her and she stood transfixed again, thinking the hunger she read was not for food.

"Maybe just something to drink."

"I'll get you some ice chips. If they don't bother your stomach, I'll make you some broth."

"Sounds good."

She fled the room, anxious to escape this disturbing man. She needed to collect her thoughts.

Jessie hurried to the combination dining room/kitchen that held a large maple table with eight matching chairs, only one of which she ever used.

Jessie exhaled a long shuttering breath, still feeling anxious and uneasy. Was she making a mistake?

The phone, mounted on the wall by the front door, rang, nearly causing her to jump out of her skin. She gave a shriek and then pressed her hand over her mouth as she dashed across the room and lifted the handset.

"Hello?"

Her mother's voice added instantly to her anxiety.

"I just got off the phone with Phyllis Darby, whose son runs the kennels at Dr. Brand's. He said you brought in a sick wolf."

Jessie closed her eyes and tried to think. Her mother hated wolves above all else.

"Jessie?" The clipped, angry tone of her mother's voice forced her to speak.

"Not sick. Injured."

"What were you thinking? Have them put it down."

Jessie's stomach cramped. "Can't. They stitched him up and I let him go."

"He'll be back after your horses. You best put out some poison."

"That's illegal, Mom."

She heard her mother make a harrumphing sound. "If your father were here, I'd send him over with his rifle."

Thankfully, her dad was away at a community building project until Thursday and her mother did not drive.

"An injured wolf is more dangerous than a healthy one. If he kills your neighbor's stock, it will be your responsibility. You're supposed to help protect your neighbors, not cause them more grief."

"I know, Mom."

Her mother gave her the silent treatment for a few moments. Jessie clenched the phone, refusing to explain further.

"I'll call you when Daddy gets home. Call me if that wolf comes back."

"Okay. Bye, Mom."

Her mother's goodbye was as cool as November breezes. Jessie pressed the button to disconnect, then hit it again and dialed the veterinarian's office, as she promised, reporting that the patient was awake, doing fine and that his master had picked him up.

She returned the handset to the cradle, then sagged against the counter before the kitchen windows. It took a moment to put the conversation with her mother behind her. When she pushed off from the counter and lifted her attention to the window, she was met with the sight of her horses, grazing peacefully in the pasture across the road.

Everything looked the same, except for the debris scattered by her guest's landing. Small branches, still holding their leaves, and dead wood littered her yard. The blue plastic tarp had blown off her woodpile.

But Little Biscuit, Custer and Apple Blossom all belied the whirlwind her life had suddenly become. They nipped at the grass as they moved steadily on, pausing only to whisk their tails to brush off a particularly persistent fly.

Seeing them usually calmed her spirit, but not today. They could not draw her from the realization that her neat little world seemed suddenly to be listing badly to one side. Like a boat taking on water, everything she believed now seemed in danger of capsizing and taking her along to the bottom.

But if the teachings were wrong about the Skin-walker's intelligence, illiteracy, lifestyle…what else was wrong?

Jessie had believed everything her mother had told her—until now.

Now she was uncertain, confused…lost.

Chapter 7

Nick watched her approach. She crept forward, arm extended, as if offering an unfamiliar dog a bone. He had an irrational impulse to growl at her. It was hard not to be in full possession of himself. When had he last depended on another soul?

Never. All his one hundred and twenty-eight years life he had lived by his wit and his strength. Until now. Now he wasn't even strong enough to leave.

Not that he wanted to. He found Jessie Healy fascinating. She was not at all the kind of woman he pursued. She was too bright, too dedicated to her work and far too disenchanted with him. But there was something beyond her lovely face and beautiful honey-colored eyes that made him wish he was healthy enough to make a move. After all, he was injured, but not dead. Any man with breath still in him would find her attractive. She was slim and curvy with flaring hips that swayed as she crossed the carpet to him. She dressed to hide her breasts in a loose-fitting blouse, but the tight jeans, Maka be praised. They did improve the view.

She stood over him now, seducing him with her fragrance. He could smell everything, from the floral dryer sheet she used on her blouse to the spearmint breath mint now in her mouth. But mostly he smelled her, spicy and floral all at once. She did not douse herself in perfume, as many women did. Her personal scent was far more arousing than such creations.

He accepted the cup of ice, lifted a fractured cube and sucked it. Her reaction told him he hadn't lost all his charm. She stared at his mouth with wide eyes and open mouth; then recalling herself, she glanced away. But it was too late. The chemistry of her body changed, her flash of desire as tangible to him as the fragrance of roses.

Her reaction did wonders for his outlook. He continued to suck on the ice, letting the cold water he extracted cool his dry throat. He rested for a time, feeling the heat of her gaze upon him, listening for the slight rustle of her clothing as she retreated.

He opened his eyes to find her already at the door, clutching the knob, as if she might need to slam it during her retreat.

"How's your stomach?" she whispered.

"Perfect."

"That's good. If you'll excuse me. I have to go see to the horses." She turned tail and fled.

"Horses, my ass." Nick smiled. "Run away while you can, little rabbit."

She left him a long time, poking her head into his room after the daylight was nearly gone. He could tell from the way she cocked her head to listen that it was too dark for her to see him. But he could see everything, including the slight dampness of sweat clinging to the skin visible at the opening of her blouse. She smelled of sweet hay and the musky tang of horses.

"Are you awake?" she whispered.

He liked the sound.

"Yes."

She startled. "How's your stomach?"

"Growling."

She lifted her eyebrows and then flicked on the light. "I'll fix you something."

He watched her hasty retreat. She'd have to venture near to bring him food, wouldn't she?

A few minutes later she returned, she carried a tray with chamomile tea, broth and toast. He kept his eyes closed to encourage her approach. When she reached his bedside, he opened his eyes. She froze and the tray tipped dangerously. She righted it before dousing him with hot tea.

He pushed himself to a sitting position, stifling a groan. Instead, he inhaled, smelling the lemon soap she used to wash her hands. "Smells good."

She lowered the tray to the side table, being careful not to get too close to him, and then retreated to the opposite side of the room as swiftly as possible.

Nick's smirk told Jessie he knew she was skittish

as a colt scenting a coyote. Now that he was alert, he scared her. And until she knew the truth, she'd keep her distance. He was wounded, but his earlier stunt proved he was still far stronger than she was.

Nick reached for a slice of toast. The medicine seemed to be working, but still he took shallow breaths, which made him seem as much wolf as man.

Why then did she have trouble taking her eyes off him? *Curiosity,* she told herself. For with his face swollen and discolored, he certainly wasn't easy on the eye, except for that perfect mouth. She couldn't take her eyes off it. The sensual curl, the full lower lip and the slight indent in the skin below it. It was the most tempting mouth she'd ever seen and one of the few places not damaged by the attack.

She could leave now, but she sat rooted to her place, fascination battling with her survival instinct.

He chewed the toast and took a swig of tea and made a face.

She smiled. "It's chamomile to settle your stomach and it's herbal."

He eyed the yellow liquid suspiciously, then took another tentative swallow. He was an oddity, a real Skinwalker, and she had him here, captive, after a fashion. She could ask him things that had always puzzled her.

Just don't expect him to tell the truth. She heard the voice in her head as clearly as if her mother had spoken the words and wondered again if her mom had already picked up some vibe about her houseguest.

"Tastes good." Nick popped the last crust of toast

into his alluring mouth and then hoisted the soup bowl, glancing around. "No spoon?"

She felt her cheeks heat as she realized she had assumed he wouldn't know how to use one.

Nick seemed to recognize her oversight was not an oversight at all. But he smiled. "I'm also house-broken."

"I'm so sorry. I just never... I don't." She rose. "I'll be right back."

She made it to the kitchen, where she rested her head on the cool refrigerator door. His voice did something to her and that teasing... Why did he have to be charming?

She retrieved the silverware and a linen napkin and returned to him. "I don't have many houseguests."

He accepted the spoon.

She watched him and realized he had better manners than she did, dipping the spoon from the front of the bowl and moving it away from him before bringing the mouthful to his lips.

He finished what he could but did not lift the bowl to drain the last drop, as she often did.

Nick raised his attention to her and grinned. "Expecting me to lick the bowl?"

She felt her neck and cheeks grow hot. "Not at all."

He lifted one brow, showing his disbelief, and they shared a smile. Hers died first.

"You weren't there, were you?" she asked.

"Where?" he asked.

"The war?"

He flinched as if she had slapped him and glanced

into the empty bowl as he slowly shook his head. Why wouldn't he meet her eye?

"I was a child then. With my mother."

"Was she a…"

"A Skinwalker? No. Human. Fleetfoot's exception to the rule. He hunted humans but somehow mated with one. A mistake that cost him his life."

"Never heard that." *Perhaps because it isn't true.* Jessie leaned toward him, feeling the tension between them and something else. Why did he follow her every move with such interest? "I don't know if I should believe you."

"Truce was signed by both sides. The war is over."

"Not to some."

Nick set aside the tray and stifled a yawn.

"You should rest. Do you want something to help you sleep?" She did not wait for his answer but brought him two bottles. "This one is your pain medication and this one is one of mine, to help you sleep."

He didn't like her sudden animation. What was she up to?

"Thanks."

"Call if you need me."

She scooped up the tray and practically ran from the room.

Nagi finished with the woman and left her in the tangled sheets. He was not certain what would come from the night's work. Unlike his fellow spirits, his body lacked a certain corporality. Bedding the woman required possession, and he was not sure if the offspring would be his or his host's.

Time would tell.

Now he would seek another womb that was ripe and fertile and then another. After all, a farmer does not sow one grain of wheat.

When his race of Halfling ghosts was born, he would be unstoppable. His race would rule them all.

But first, he needed to find replacements to guard the wolf. He had many able ghosts in his circle, but if he released them, Hihankara, the old viper, was sure to sound the alarm. Evil souls never left his circle once they crossed unless it was to enter the Spirit World and then out if they were redeemed by the prayers of the living, in any case, they could not cross to the physical plane without his help and the crone's notice. Soon it would not matter. But for the time being, he had to keep his plans secret.

He abandoned his host and took to the sky, turning back just in time to see the man fall like wet cement to the floor of the garage. His purpose served, Nagi left him where he lay to hunt the earth for strong, ruthless ghosts clever enough to outwit a wounded wolf.

As he journeyed over the land, he kept an eye open for an Inanoka. If he happened upon one, he could try wounding it in hopes it knew the bear. He wondered if he could again stir the hostilities between Niyanoka and Inanoka. The two Halfling races hated each other and their truce was fragile. It would not take much to bring them to war again. On the other hand, the Inanoka might serve as allies if he left the animals alone. Perhaps they would see the elimination of man as a boon. After all, many had once thought so and the species had only grown more destructive in the interim.

Either way, he knew the guardians of humans would surely stand between him and his aim. It was the duty of every Spirit Child to protect man.

This was why he could not fathom the reason the Thunderbirds had taken a wounded Skinwalker to his born enemy. And who could have predicted a Dream Walker would shelter him. The Thunderbirds, obviously, he realized. Why hadn't the Niyanoka killed him?

There was a reason, but he was missing some vital detail. What was it?

It did not bode well. If these two could set aside their old grievances, their people might do the same.

The wolf had found an unlikely ally. But his ghosts could remove the Dream Walker and that would leave the wolf with only two choices—seek the Healer or die.

The first ghost arrived alone. He traveled through the wall and paused before the wolf. This one had strong sexual energy; it beat in a low throb even as he rested, calling to the female in a sweet song just below her hearing. But the woman felt it. Already her own pulsing beat began to change, answering his call, connecting them with invisible threads.

His predecessors had done their work well. The wolf's body was broken and torn, but still he was a Skinwalker and not to be underestimated.

The Dream Walker had used Western medicine to

heal him, instead of her own powers. Did she not know her gifts could heal more than the mind?

Not that it mattered to him that the wolf suffered. The ghost did not mind another's torment. But he did prefer pleasure. He had lived as a hedonist, satisfying his unique tastes mostly with children, young ones especially, and had been so adept that he was never brought to justice, not to human justice, at least.

But now Nagi had found him. Instead of judgment, he'd been offered redemption. It was better than he could have ever imagined—a chance he would not squander.

He had been a voyeur in life. As a ghost, he found this habit much easier. The wolf did not perceive him. What about the woman? She had powers of sight, but was not a Seer. Still, he would keep clear of her when possible.

He would wait outside of her house, unless he sensed some disturbance.

Chapter 8

Jessie peered into his room before retiring and found Nick lying on his back with his eyes closed. His breathing was slow and relaxed and she noted the cap off the painkillers. What surprised her was the realization that she still found herself intimidated by him even when he was sleeping. She let her gaze wander from his thick black hair and over his brutalized face to the thick corded muscles at his throat. He had left his shirt unbuttoned and it was flipped back on one side, revealing his magnificent chest. Earlier she had been too embarrassed to look, but she did so now and felt her heart beat faster.

She had been around ranchers and cattlemen much of her long life and had had many opportunities to see young men shirtless as they went about their work. But never in all her ninety-seven years had she seen the chiseled perfection of this man's chest and abdomen. The smooth skin and thick muscle were broken only by the blue and purple bruising over his ribs. She winced. That must have hurt. The center of the bruising was punctuated by a small white bandage over the incision.

She felt sorry for his pain and that surprised her. It seemed the hatred her mother had injected into her only daughter was not as strong as her empathy for a man in pain.

He turned his head and winced, drawing his breath through clenched teeth. She took only one step into the room before his eyes snapped open and fixed on her. The muscles of his stomach tensed and she caught her breath at the sensual sight.

"How you feeling?" she asked, embarrassed at the strange strained quality of her voice and the tingling sensation rippling over her skin. It reminded her of the electrical charge of the air before a lightning strike.

"Better."

He didn't look it. She smiled and lifted the full glass of water as if it was her admission ticket. Then she gathered her flagging courage and crossed the room, setting the glass beside his bed, next to the medicine. "In case you don't want to chew them."

She leaned down to flicked off the light beside him. He watched her every move with such an intent stare, it made her nervous. Next she turned off the overhead light, leaving only the small lamp on the desk glowing dimly because of the large stained-glass shade. Then she backed away until she collided with the reading chair across the room, fell back into the familiar cushions, leaping up again as if scorched.

Why was she suddenly so clumsy?

He continued to stare.

"I wanted to be sure you didn't need anything else. Before I, uh, head to bed."

His eyes were distrustful. She remembered the pillow, now under his head.

"Rest," she urged.

He didn't. "I'm a very light sleeper." He glanced at the water and inhaled.

"Don't be so suspicious. I'm not trying to poison you."

"Because I could smell it if you tried."

She couldn't keep her mouth from dropping open. "Really?"

He gave a slight incline of his head. He stared long enough to make her truly uncomfortable and then turned his head and closed his eyes. She crept from the room.

When she checked on him an hour later, she made it to the chair beside her desk, and he did not seem to rouse, though his breathing changed. She did not venture closer, fearing he'd wake, but instead settled in her comfortable chair.

She closed her eyes to meditate. She was attuned to dreamers and so knew that her appearance had roused him, but not quite to consciousness. She had been wise not to draw any closer. She felt the moment when he relaxed back into slumber and exactly when his first dream began.

From her meditative state Jessie released her astral

self from her body, freeing her spirit to seek the wolf. Vicinity did ease in location and she found him quickly, surprising even herself. Her entrance to his dream caused barely a ripple, and has much more gentle than with most of her human clients.

She found herself standing beneath the shelter of the wide branches of a huge pine, which hid her in shadows. Jessie looked out on a sunny grotto, surrounded by evergreens on three sides and a rocky cliff face on the fourth. For some reason the area radiated power, like a holy place. There before her, below the altar of rock, stood a woman with long dark hair pulled back at her nape. She wore a loose cotton dress that flowed over her ripe body, revealing herself to be at the final stages of a pregnancy. From the look of her, she would deliver very soon. Beside the expectant mother stood a giant of a man, dressed like Paul Bunyan in red flannel and dark blue jeans. His earthy aura marked him as a Skinwalker, while the woman cast a bright golden light that said unmistakably she was one of Jessie's people.

The Seer and the Healer.

Here were the two Nicholas had told her about. So they did exist, and they glowed with life. Somehow Nicholas had managed to contact his friends, but would they remember his visit upon waking?

Jessie always did, but it was her gift to speak to the living in dreams. Her grandmother had the gift of contacting the dead. Thus far, Jessie had been unable to reach anyone who had crossed to the Spirit Road.

But where was Nicholas? She knew this place and these people could not exist here without him. The

Healer glanced about and found the large gray wolf, standing so still he was nearly imperceptible among the trees.

He approached them from the opposite direction. The large man saw him first, or rather smelled him, his nose twitching as he turned.

Silly mistake to approach a Skinwalker from downwind…or was it a mistake? Somehow she doubted it.

The woman followed the direction of her mate's gaze and her arms went up in surprise as a smile blossomed on her face.

"Nicholas!"

The wolf paused, sat and curled his tail around his paws.

She moved slowly, but with grace. "Transform this instant so I can give you a hug."

He did.

Jessie gasped at what she saw. He stood tall and strong, without a hint of the cracked ribs that had rounded his shoulders. His thick black hair curled about his face was not bloody or swollen. No stitches crossed his nose and cheek.

His face took her breath away, for it was too beautiful to be believed. *Such a face should be illegal,* she thought at the sight of his strong jaw and cleft chin, his mouth now only the punctuation to compelling eyes and elegant nose.

His appearance made her stomach drop, her heart hammer painfully in her chest and her skin flushed as blood rushed through dilating blood vessels. He had not even looked at her and she wanted him. Never in her life had she experienced such a visceral reaction to a man. Her breathing came in gasps as she realized in that instant that he was more dangerous than she ever thought, because her reaction gave him power over her.

"What news?" asked the woman, drawing back from the gentle hug.

The man gave his welcome by thumping Nick on the shoulder with enough force to knock him momentarily off balance, which he gracefully regained an instant later. She knew such a blow should have buckled his knees.

But not him. In his dream Nicholas was whole, virile and sexy as hell.

"Bad news." Nick and the other Skinwalker exchanged a look. "I was attacked by ghosts."

"Nicholas, do you need us?" asked the Seer.

"No!" The force of the rejection took them both by surprise. "I mean, it's not necessary. I'm with a…"

How would he describe her?

"A friend."

A lie.

"She's taking care of me. It's not serious."

More lies, but spoken to protect his friends.

"They were using me as bait to reach you."

"How did they find you?" asked the Skinwalker.

Nicholas glanced away.

"You were in those damned clubs, right?"

"Not all of us can live on love alone. Some of us need…variety."

Jessie scowled. Just how much variety did Nick generally get? She was certain he'd have as much as he liked and it irritated her to find herself among the legions of enthralled females. Curse that face again.

The man lowered his chin and scowled.

The woman rested a hand on the Healer's chest and he instantly lost his grim expression. Jessie felt her breath catch at the look of tenderness he gave her. His hand circled her back, protective—possessive.

The Healer glanced back at Nick. "Are you sure you are all right?"

Nicholas smiled fondly at her and Jessie felt a sharp twinge. What the hell was that? A sinking sensation followed as Jessie correctly identified her reaction as jealousy.

"Pathetic," she whispered.

"What should we do?" asked the woman to her mate.

"We keep moving, keep to the wild. Nagi can't find us unless a ghost spots us. So we stay away from people, that's all we can do for now."

"But what about Nick?"

The Skinwalker rested a protective hand on his mate's swollen belly and her protests died.

"Keep safe, Nicholas, and thank you for telling us," said the Healer.

The woman rested her hand on her belly and grimaced. "I swear, my bladder has shrunk to the size of a peanut. I never sleep through the night anymore." She turned to her mate. "Come, love."

Hand in hand the two strolled toward the rock, disappearing into a slicing crevice.

Nick watched them go, then turned and looked directly at Jessie.

Jessie shrank back, even knowing she could not be seen unless she chose to be seen. But still he stared.

His roguish smile spread across his wide mouth. "You can come out now, Dream Walker."

Jessie's heart nearly stopped.

Chapter 9

Jessie had entered hundreds, no thousands, of dreams but never had she felt so exposed. What was happening?

He had seen her. It made no difference, for he would not recall their tête-à-tête.

No one ever did.

Even when she chose to be seen, her time here would be washed away by his waking, like footprints at low tide. And he posed no danger to her here. Even a Tracker, with his superior strength, could not trap a Dream Walker. She could leave at anytime and nothing he could do could detain her. Here *she* had the advantage.

Gathering her resolve, she stepped into the clearing.

Nicholas extended his hand, and for reasons she did not wish to closely examine, she took it.

The contact brought instant heat to her skin.

Nick captured Jessie's other hand; his hold was gentle, yet commanding. The joy on his face took her breath away.

"You're here."

He was tall and as straight as an oak, with broad shoulders, lithe, agile muscles and a face that promised both peace and chaos.

"I wanted to see…" Her words fell off.

"If I was lying." He finished for her. "I know."

"You…"

He smiled. "You're in the room right now. I heard you come in."

He knew what she was up to and still he allowed this intrusion. It pointed to a clear conscience.

She bowed her head and changed the subject. "Was that the Healer and the Seer of Souls?"

He glanced in the direction the couple had gone. "Yes."

"They seem very much in love."

"For now."

She was surprised by the pessimism in his tone, as if it was inevitable that their relationship would fail.

"You don't think their love will last?" she asked.

He made a little growling noise in the back of his throat. "I've never seen love last. Mostly such pairings end badly and they face more challenges than most." Then he gave her a charming smile that she thought masked his true emotions. "Perhaps they are the exception to the rule."

"Why are you so cynical?"

"I prefer realistic. There is no worse trap than the

unnatural bond between male and female. Such liaisons are meant to last as long as it takes to safely raise young. Sometimes not even that long."

Jessie didn't know what to say to that. It was the most unromantic thing she'd ever heard.

"What about love?"

He released her hands and stepped away.

"A very dangerous illusion. To love is to give unlimited power to another person. Without love you do not have jealousy, betrayal or the lust for revenge."

Jessie stared at him, completely speechless. Where could he have gotten such bleak beliefs? She thought of her own parents and a nasty suspicion rose. It took her father, a peacemaker, over a half century to convince her mother to have a child. Her mother, who was a Dream Walker like Jessie, having survived the war, did not think it fit to bring a baby into this world. Jessie was their only child.

Nick's father was Fleetfoot. What lessons of love had he gleaned from the most notorious Skinwalker of them all? She thought of what she knew of his father. All but one of his warriors had been killed at Blood Creek. Only his second in command had escaped justice. It was said that Fleetfoot had come to a meeting with her people to discuss a surrender but then attacked one of the ambassadors. His capture went badly and many of her people died as heroes.

How had the story been told to Nick?

"You said you were too young to fight in the war. But do you remember your father?"

Nick's expression grew dark as he folded his arms before him in a move dripping with obstinacy.

"I do not talk of this." He glared at her. "Not to anyone. Not ever."

She was used to such resistance. It never lasted. "Think of me as the exception to your rule. How did you know of your father?"

He raked his hands through his thick hair and she knew he would tell her. "I was there when he was taken. My mother brought me. I was two."

Her eyes rounded. What had he seen?

"My mother called him a monster." Nick gave her a look of such open anguish, she felt her heart break in two. "What does that make me?"

"Oh, Nick."

He glanced away and sat upon the mossy ground, then indicated the place beside him. She settled in the soft loam and watched him as he lifted his gaze to the treetops. Somewhere nearby a spring gurgled with life.

"It doesn't look bloody here now," he said.

Jessie looked around at the peaceful clearing, unable to contain her shock. This was Blood Creek? "Here?"

"It is where they first met, where they first made love and where I was conceived." He pressed his hands deep into the springy moss, as if feeling their passion. "She didn't know what he was then. She was in love with a handsome man who promised to take her away. It was all she cared about. After I was born and she discovered what he was, her love died a bitter death. And yes, this is also the place where your people met my father. She chose it. Ironic, isn't it? The place of her surrender and then of his. She was the only one who could have lured him out in the open. That is the power of love."

Jessie picked up the familiar story. "He came because he learned how many more humans there were in the East and that no one could kill them all."

He stared at her, his brow dipping over his eyes. "Is that what they taught you in your schools?"

She nodded.

"He came to rescue us, only to find his wife was a willing participant in the Niyanoka plot."

"He attacked John Painter."

"Who had a knife to my throat. My mother handed me over to him as bait, right after she told me she wouldn't raise another monster like him."

Jessie gasped. "Sweet Mystery. She tried to kill her own son."

He sat there, defiant and proud. Only his eyes revealed the agony.

"I'm so sorry, Nick."

"I don't want your pity."

"It wasn't your fault," she insisted.

"Wasn't it? He never would have come if not for me. He died saving his only son. He knew it was a trap. He still came—for me." Nick's eyes glittered and he looked away. "He fought well."

She was shocked speechless. She'd never heard this, and here, in his dream, she knew he told her the absolute truth.

"He brought me to his trusted friend, a member of

his pack. Then he turned to face them, giving us time to escape."

"They killed him."

He nodded. "Gone because he once loved a woman who used that power to destroy him."

No wonder he had such feelings about love and marriage, with such a tragic history as his first lesson. If he kept people away, they couldn't use him. What an empty existence.

"Did you ever see your mother again?"

His eyes glittered with sorrow and rage. "I was raised by my own kind."

She could not think of what to say. "Not all love affairs end so badly."

His response was flat and cold. "Especially if they are brief."

"It was a bloody war."

"Not so bloody as the one waged between a woman and man."

"If you don't approve of love, then why were you with those women?"

"I make love to them. There's a difference." Something caught his attention. "There he is."

Cold fear washed her and she moved behind Nick, seeking protection even as her mind told her she could escape.

There on the rise, standing on a rock outcropping, was a large male timber wolf, the largest she had ever seen. His left ear was tattered. She recognized him instantly—Fleetfoot.

"Make him go away," she whispered, gripping his sleeve.

The wolf turned and disappeared. She knew it was only a creation of Nick's mind, but still it terrified her.

"He's gone."

She stayed where she was, trembling and clinging as if this were her nightmare. He gathered her up in his arms, cradling her tenderly. She had the irrational feeling that he would protect her and keep her safe—that she was home.

"What did he do to your family?" Nick asked.

She had heard the story so often, she could imagine that dreadful day. "He attacked my mother's family riding with Chivington at Sand Creek. My grandmother was killed and her father and his three brothers. They were just boys. My mother escaped to the river. She pretended to be dead, lying among the bodies of her clan. She saw everything. It has shaped her life, her beliefs."

"She hates my kind."

Jessie nodded.

"I can't blame her. But the truce has lasted. There have been no more attacks on men by my people."

"Yes, but her distrust runs deep."

"I understand that."

There were many Inanoka with Fleetfoot, but he was the most savage, sparing none, from the youngest to the oldest.

"After that, we left our clans and moved to live among the humans. They married humans to give their children a better chance at survival."

"Did you witness this?"

"No. But Fleetfoot's name was mentioned often. He was the bogeyman of my childhood."

"Yet he was butchered defending his son."

He held her, this descendant of her enemy.

"Well, he is gone from this world and will never come again. Hush now."

She did not know she was weeping until he lifted her chin and wiped away the tracks of her tears.

He held her with a combination of contained strength and tenderness that made her heart ache.

She had a moment's chagrin until she recalled he would not remember her intrusion into his dreams. But it gave her a freedom she had never fully considered.

A rapid firing of ideas bombarded her. She was with him, could be with him without consequences. She could do anything, *they* could do anything and he would not recall what had passed between them, because nothing would happen. She wasn't really here; she was back in the chair, sitting across the room from her patient. He was sleeping soundly, sedated, in his bed.

"Jessie?"

She gazed up at him, allowed herself the pleasure of appreciating the rugged cliffs of his cheek and jaw, the sharp nose that descended straight as a ski slope.

She gazed at his hypnotic blue eyes, husky eyes, wolf eyes, and sighed.

His lips twitched and then broke into a lazy, seductive smile, as if he knew her thoughts. It was as clear as the deep dimples that marked his cheeks, as clear as the strong white teeth and the new possessiveness of his grip.

Once more she stopped to consider, assuring herself that it was safe. He would not know.... No one would.

Jessie returned the smile. Everything was understood between them. His hand snaked up to cradle the nape of her neck, guiding her into position to receive his kiss.

She closed her eyes and waited.

His lips were velvet, soft as a whisper as they swept over hers. He nipped at her bottom lip and she kissed him with all the forbidden frenzy he stirred in her soul.

The ferocity of her kiss seemed to startle him for he tensed for just an instant and then tightened his hold upon her as he matched her sensual assault. Their tongues slid over one another, strong, lithe muscles stroking their desire.

He caressed her back, descending to the very base of her spine and then pressing them together at the hips.

She gasped at the electric energy of their connection and the pulsing ache that grew with each frenzied kiss.

Jessie drew back to tug away her prim blouse, flipping it inside out as she tossed it away. She wore only a lacy pink bra and jeans. He dipped a finger beneath the waistband, releasing the rivet, stripping her out of the formfitting denim.

She stood in her bra and panties, waiting impatiently as he drew his T-shirt over his head. He was nearly hairless, which allowed her to appreciate the rippling pectorals, which bunched and corded as he freed himself of his shirt. He stood still for her perusal. She let her gaze devour him.

Wide, muscular shoulders, rippling six-pack abs and narrow hips all pleased her. He was virile, predatory and dangerous.

The type of man she would never consider in her life. He would be too unpredictable, too demanding. She gazed into his hungry eyes. Yes, and too possessive, as well. But here she was safe and free to admit to herself that she wanted to be hunted, possessed and devoured. And Nick looked more than willing to make her fantasy come true.

He grasped her shoulders and dragged her forward, pressing her to his bare torso. The contact was wonderful and terrible. The warm skin and hard muscle did things to her. Her breasts ached and her nipples contracted into painful buds. She relished the contact but found it lacking. His jeans, her bra, they suddenly seemed the most infuriating of barriers.

His mouth found her neck, drawing a groan of pleasure from her lips. He worked down the column of her throat, nipping, sucking and kissing his way along, following a scent trail and marking his territory.

His attention drew the velvety moisture from her, making her grow slick and impatient. He unfastened her bra with a skill that should have given her pause. In other circumstances, she would be jealous of his past lovers, but here, now, she was grateful to be the beneficiary of his experience.

He kissed the swell at the outer edge of her breast, teasing her by not satisfying her need to feel his hot mouth draw on her. He was not rash or young and showed the maddening control of a skilled athlete.

His broad hands splayed across her rib cage as he moved circuitously toward his destination. Finally, she could stand it no longer and twisted so as to bring her nipple in contact with his lips. He breathed hot air upon her in what she thought might be a silent laugh. Did he find her wild desire for him gratifying, amusing? Did it make her just like all the others?

That disturbing thought was shaken from her mind an instant later, when his tongue flicked over her taunt nipple. The hot pinpoint of pleasure would have buckled her knees if he was not already laying her on the soft carpet of moss. Her belly pressed against his chest as he drew her forward, taking her nipple in his mouth and sucking.

She gasped at the flood of moisture between her legs.

"Great Spirit of Man," she whispered.

He drew back, gazing down at her with hungry, knowing eyes—the eyes of a man with the certain knowledge that he would get exactly what he wanted.

"Oh, no, sweet one. Even he can't deliver you from me."

Chapter 10

Michaela Proud woke with a start. Instantly, her husband, Sebastian, roused beside her, searching their cabin for any sign of a threat.

She laid a hand upon his corded biceps. Sebastian was a Skinwalker, a great grizzly bear, and even when walking in the guise of a man, he was enormous.

"A dream," she whispered.

He flopped back onto the mattress, which he had consented to use for her sake. Given his druthers, he would rest on the floor with no more than a few furs beneath him.

He wrapped an arm about her and drew her close to his side. She felt the reassurance of his body. She breathed deep of his familiar scent, feeling her frantic heartbeat slowing to match his.

He nuzzled her hair and then kissed the top of her head. "Tell me."

"I saw Nick."

"Nick? What was he doing?" Sebastian understood the power of dreams as messengers, so it was important that she remember correctly.

She closed her eyes and tried to grasp the fleeting images as they fled. "You were there, too."

"Where?"

"At the Palisades."

He stiffened. "Near Nick's lodge."

She concentrated. "Yes."

Her husband's body was now tense and she read his thoughts. This was the place where Fleetfoot met his end. A haunted, sacred place to his people. She tried to focus on her own thoughts and not become entangled in his.

Why had Nick come? Her eyes popped open. "Ghosts."

Sebastian rolled toward her. "Where?"

It was natural for him to think there were ghosts about them, since she had the gift to both see and speak to those who had not yet walked the Spirit Road. As the last Seer of Souls, she alone could see ghosts, not in possession of a host body, and she could see all Spirits.

She stroked his cheek to calm him. "Not here."

Michaela could not see his face in the dim light cast by only the stars, but knew that he could see her clearly. He retained all his gifts when in the form of a man, night sight among the rest.

"Ghosts in your dream?" he asked.

She shook her head. "Nick saw them. They attacked him!"

"Ghosts cannot attack a living creature."

"He was attacked. I could sense death lingering about him."

Sebastian sat up. "Is Nick dead?"

"No, no." She assured him by pushing him back into his place beside her. "But he has been touched by them."

Sebastian thought on this. "Possession?"

"It must be. But ghosts can not possess an Inanoka. I don't understand what happened but something did. We should go to him."

"Did he ask us to go to him?"

She closed her eyes, trying to recall his exact words. Her eyes popped open. "Bait. He said something about bait."

"What does that mean?"

It all flooded back to her. "They are using him to find you and thus find me."

Sebastian's voice growled. "Nagi."

Her husband pressed his cheek to the top of her head, cradling her close.

She said nothing but wrapped her arms protectively about her swollen belly, trying to ward off the chill that even her husband's strong arms could not dispel.

"Tomorrow we go farther north."

"What about Nick?"

Sebastian's voice held a tension she recognized as

worry, although she knew it would appear as callousness to one who did not know him. "He's a wolf. He can take care of himself."

Nicholas stroked his tongue across Jessie's ripe pink nipple, glorying in the cries of excitement she gave. They were like fuel to his internal fires.

This wild, beautiful and passionate Spirit Child had consented to have him. He did not question it.

This woman, Jessie, she did something to him, something new. The urgency, for one thing. He used all his control not to rush to take what she offered. A sheen of sweat covered them now, adding to the fragrance of arousal and the glide of skin on skin.

He moved lower, kissing the velvet of her stomach as he peeled away the scrap of lace that kept him from her.

The nest of dark, tight curls and the moan of anticipation spurred him. He dipped a finger into her honeyed cleft and kissed her as she arched toward him. He kissed and licked as his fingers moved within her. With the other hand he stroked her from the sensitive mound of her breast to the silky skin of her inner thigh. She moved as gracefully as the ocean, rhythmic and eternal.

She reached her first climax as he kissed her, gasping out his name. He closed his eyes to savor the sweetness of her surrender. Then he brushed his mouth against her inner thigh, to remove the moisture that clung there, and scaled her body like an explorer.

She splayed her legs as he settled between her thighs,

poised to take her. Their gazes met, hers sleepy and sultry, his, no doubt, hungry. The smile she gave him both satisfied and aroused. In it she promised him pleasure, but something more; he knew it was more. This joining, though new, seemed familiar, as if he should remember her, them.

He brushed aside the odd rumination and grasped her hips.

"You're sweet as honey," he whispered. Who would have expected such passion from a Spirit Child? This was a side of her personality she had kept hidden, this passion and this heat.

She threaded her fingers in his hair and drew him forward for a kiss, thrusting her tongue into his mouth as he thrust into her.

She cried out and fell back, arching to meet him. The slide of his turgid flesh against her soft folds made him groan in pleasure. The bump of his hips to her pelvis signaled their joining. He paused there and then drew back. Despite the intimate connection, he needed the connection of her gaze, needed to see if she felt the uniqueness of this.

In his time on earth, he had slept with many women, too many to count. He could not say exactly what was different, but recognized it just the same. Her anticipation of his needs, his ability to make her lose her reserve and the complete honesty of this moment all struck him.

He gazed at her, seeing her for the first time as she truly was, ripe, real and passionate. She wanted him, wanted this. He knew she was not like him, randy and promiscuous.

That she had accepted him, allowed him entrance into her body was nearly unfathomable.

And then he realized what was different, the reason for his added pleasure, the cause of his increased arousal.

He was not just guessing at her feelings. He knew them. Felt them as clearly as he experienced his own.

What was this?

The shock of his realization caused him to draw back. It was a mistake, the straw on the camel, the step too far.

He felt the quickening inside her as her climax threatened. The rolling wave of pleasure merged with his own. Together they were unstoppable.

He surged forward again, gripping her as if to keep himself from falling. He was falling. She lifted her hips and arched her back, opening to his thrusts.

Her cries mingled with his long groan of release as they toppled into a crashing ecstasy, a waterfall of tumbling, tumult that tangled their limbs together.

His body jolted awake, the wave of pleasure dissolving into the jagged pain of his waking reality. His face burned, his ribs pulsed with agony and...oh, sweet mother of us all, he glanced down at his crotch. He hadn't had a wet dream for nearly a hundred years.

His gaze lifted to the light across the room and found Jessie sitting in the armchair. One elbow perched on the armrest, allowing her hand to cradle her cheek. Her eyes were closed but blinked open as he stared.

She gasped as their eyes met.

Jessie straightened in the chair. What had happened?

One minute she was deep inside his dream and the next…

She stared across the room at Nick. He glared at her, his jaw so tight the muscle bulged.

If she didn't know better—the realization swept past her like a retreating tide. No, no, it wasn't possible.

He kept his gaze intent, accusatory.

He *couldn't* remember; no one *ever* remembered.

But she'd never tried her dream walking on an Inanoka. So she really didn't know.

Jessie stiffened as the certainty petrified her. He knew.

"What did you do?" he growled.

Her jaw dropped as words failed her. Sweet Maka, help her. What *had* she done? In his dream he was so handsome, so giving. The temptation and promise of anonymity were too much to resist and she had lowered her guard.

"Oh, Great Spirit," she whispered.

"You invaded my dream."

"I never thought that…I mean, I didn't intend…" How could she finish?

"You didn't intend to get caught. Is that what you didn't intend? 'Cause you sure as hell had no qualms about stroking me up one side and down the other."

"Nicholas, please." She'd never used his given name before. But now that she had seen him whole and beautiful, the battered creature before her had ceased to be. She needed to recall who he was, no, *what* he was. But all she could do was hum like a struck piano chord. Her body still trembled from his lovemaking.

The moisture of her wanting slickened her panties and she shifted uncomfortably. "I just wanted to find the truth."

"And you found it. The truth is you are just like the rest of them. You want me for only one thing."

What did he mean, the rest? She could not think with her mind spinning. She had never, ever taken advantage of a sleeper. She suddenly felt sickened by what she had done.

"Do you do this often? Sneak into men's dreams and strip down like a pole dancer?"

She sprang to her feet in a wave of indignation. "Never! I didn't intend for that to happen."

"The hell you didn't, What a joke. You really had me fooled, all aloof on the exterior, but oh my, how you burn underneath." His groan was deep and sensual. "I've never felt anything like that. You're damn good, Doc. What exactly did you do?"

"I don't know. I just wanted to find out about the Seer. I don't understand this any better than you do."

"Well, you have your answers." He let his head fall back to the pillow, as if suddenly exhausted. "Sweet mother, you could have killed me."

"You were safe here in bed the whole time," she said as she crept to the door.

He gave a disparaging snort and then grimaced.

"It never really happened," she insisted.

He met her stare with a quirking smile that radiated confidence and an aura bright with sexuality.

"Keep telling yourself that, Doc. But we both know the truth."

Her chin sunk to her chest. "I'm sorry, Nicholas. It won't happen again."

"No? Why the hell not? We were perfect together, too damned perfect."

Perfect, he said. Yes, that was how it had felt to her as well—the draw, the need, the connection. It had beaten between them like a living thing. If not for the bandages, the cuts, the fractures, she might be inching toward him even now.

Oh, no, she couldn't. He was Inanoka, for the love of all the Spirits. Forbidden forever.

Yet she had bitten the apple and wanted—no, needed—another bite. How could she ever go back to the way things were before? The magnitude of her mistake sent her fleeing for the sanctuary of her bedroom. Behind her she thought she heard laughter, followed by a pitiful groan.

Chapter 11

Nick started after her and then stopped. His confusion made him hesitate, preventing him from pursuit. He'd made love to many women, but this experience was unique. The magnitude of his response gave him pause. He had never cared about anything this much. That meant he needed to be cautious. For despite his hard words, something about Jessie was different than all the others and that made her dangerous.

She had shown him a completely different side.

In his dream she was sensual and arousing. She took what she wanted and spoke her mind. He liked that and found himself drawn to her with a fearsome force.

What would it take to bring that woman into this world?

Don't be stupid. She despises you.

But her reaction to him in his dream said otherwise.

A hypocrite, then, saying one thing while doing another. Which was the truth?

Most women were attracted to his human face and form. Perhaps in this Jessie was no different, drawn in when she had seen him uninjured and whole. But he could not account for his racing thoughts. She actually made him consider possibilities that were not open to one as solitary as a wolf. Things like a future and a home.

He thought he'd forsaken that fantasy long ago and was surprised to find it clinging to him still—tenacious as a badger. Only a fool would pursue that illusion. And Nick was no fool. He was a realist who understood exactly the kind of havoc love wrought.

His mother had shown him the folly of loving humans. They were weak, fickle and short-lived. So Nick had never seen them as other than a momentary hiatus from his chosen path. Although he sometimes ran with wolves, they knew him for what he was and that kept him from truly entering a pack. That left the Inanoka, many of whom saw him as the reason their greatest leader had fallen, and the Niyanoka, who hated all of his kind. Besides, it was love that brought his father to his death. Not the love for a woman, but the love for his child, the need to protect—even at the cost of his life. He knew his friend Sebastian faced this same curse even now, trying to protect his offspring from a true Spirit. He pitied him, but did not ever plan to place himself in such a vulnerable position—not for a woman.

He'd rather face his own death than give a woman his

heart. At least there was a limit to how much suffering one could experience while dying. Not so with the pain of love.

He groaned again and closed his eyes, knowing it was not over.

There in the night, he trembled with need for her, straining his control to stay in his narrow single bed. How had she stirred this reaction? He had never ached for a woman as he ached for this one. He'd always chosen when and who, keeping the power for himself and making the engagements brief. He had never faced anything like this gnawing hunger.

Was it because she was not a woman, or at least, not only a woman? She was a Spirit Child and that was something with which he had no experience.

Perhaps she had this effect on all men. It would explain why she wore such armor against invasion. But, oh, once he found the chink and crawled inside, she was all fire and heat.

He had three broken bones and the Great Mystery only knew how many stitches, and yet the throbbing that caused the most discomfort was well south of his ribs. He wanted her again—and not just in a dream. What would he do if she didn't accept him again?

He groaned.

Nick reached for the pills she had left, seeking a few hours respite from his healing body and spinning mind. They were bitter, but it was not very long before his skin began to tingle and his eyelids sagged. The pain was still there, but disconnected somehow, as if it belonged to someone else.

"If I'm lucky, she'll come visiting again."

He slipped into a heavy sleep and did not rouse when a large black raven landed upon his windowsill. In a moment it had torn the screen away and slipped into his room.

It hopped onto the bed and strode up to his pillow, examining the line of stitches that punctured his skin. Then with loving care, it began to preen the hair that had fallen over his face. As it worked, it made a rolling caw, low in its throat, as if humming or scolding the sleeping man.

Jessie should have asked her neighbor to carry Nick to the upstairs bedrooms so he would be that much farther away. But she'd shut the heat off up there and the bedrooms were unfurnished, plus the distance from the bathroom and kitchen would have made caring for him more difficult. Just once she wished she hadn't done the practical thing, because now he lay only steps from where she slept. She briefly considered moving upstairs herself, but rejected the notion. She would not let a wolf drive her from her bedroom.

Jessie lay beneath her coverlet, resting fitfully, unable to escape from her thoughts.

Of all the dreams she had entered, never had she been remembered. Not one of her patients ever even knew she was watching. None spoke to her unless she engaged them in conversation and no one ever touched her. She had never experienced anything like this.

Her breech of ethics galled her and she could offer no defense. What she had done was wrong—so wrong.

She had never been tempted to kiss a man in a dream, had never felt that exulting freedom that comes from anonymity. She had wanted him and she had acted on impulse.

And she had been caught.

She deserved every bit of his outrage. And now things were a hundred times worse. There would be no denying her attraction to him, not when he knew the truth. Since he had first spoken to her, she had felt the unnatural hum of desire vibrating inside her, but she'd fought it. She didn't want to be attracted to a wolf.

Great Mystery, if her mother ever learned of this.... Jessie trembled, pulling the blanket up around her neck but gained no comfort. She glanced out the window and groaned.

Outside the world was black. The clock beside her bed told her it was the middle of the night, yet she could not sleep.

Her mind lay divided. Part of her wanted to sneak away and never have to face him again. Another part recalled her promise and wondered if he needed her. Did he need the bedpan or more water? Round and round her mind raced.

Perhaps she'd just hire someone to care for him, or bring him to the hospital. There was no danger he would transform now. He could heal there, safely, away from her.

But he wasn't safe from her there. She could still visit him anywhere he went. How long could she resist his allure?

Why didn't he have someone he could call, some

family member or friend? She had never met anyone who was so absolutely alone. But then she recalled why. Her people had killed his father.

She had promised him. She groaned and covered her head with the pillow, then tossed it away and resigned herself to check on her patient. She kicked viciously at the bedcovers and retrieved her robe.

The night-light in the kitchen cast a yellowish glow and provided enough light for her to reach her study. There she found her pace slowed. Maybe she shouldn't. He was a light sleeper and she might awaken him.

Coward.

If he didn't wake up, could she resist the need to visit him again?

She paused before the door as she recalled her promise to do her best for him.

Jessie stiffened her spine and entered the study, but paused as she realized what she was wearing.

She glanced down at her mismatched yellow-and-green fuzzy socks, her tattered lavender cotton nightgown and her very large men's red flannel robe, which she'd taken when her father announced his intention to throw it out.

It certainly wasn't something she'd like to have him see her in. The very fact that she even cared what he thought of her outfit, that she had for one instant considered changing into something he might find appealing, sickened her. It showed that she had no control.

Well, she would beat this thing. She was a Spirit

Child. It meant stifling her animal impulses and acting only after considerable thought.

Like you did earlier?

She balled her hands into fists, hating that little voice. Jessie clasped the doorknob and turned it very gently, cracked the door and peered inside.

The desk lamp cast enough illumination for her to see Nick, his head turned to the side, his chest uncovered and his breathing shallow. She took a step inside and registered motion near the wall.

A raven sat on the bedpost of the headboard, its sharp beak no longer tucked beneath its wing as it turned its head and fixed two bead-black eyes on her.

A bird in the house—the worst of all omens.

Jessie staggered backward, striking the door with her back and slamming it closed. Nick did not even stir. That frightened Jessie even more than the raven.

Had it killed him?

She flicked on the overhead light and then rushed forward to strike it, but the raven opened its wings and lifted into the air, landing on the back of her comfortable chair.

Jessie continued toward Nick, stroking his cheek and assuring herself that he was alive. She gazed down at the black stitches, knowing he would bear the scars the rest of his life. That, too, was her fault, for she had allowed a large-animal vet to stitch him instead of a plastic surgeon.

Jessie stood between Nick and the raven. Why was it here?

"It's just a bird," she whispered to herself.

She glanced about the room for a weapon and then spotted the torn screen. This was past bizarre—a raven flying at night and breaking into a house. She lifted a glass paperweight from her desk and hefted it like a hand grenade. It was then that she noticed the familiar brown aura glowing about the bird and something more. There was a gold glow circling its head, like a wreath. It was the mark of a spiritual creature. She had never seen this color outside of a Niyanoka.

"Son of a bitch," she muttered and lowered her weapon. She replaced the glass orb on the desktop, keeping her eyes on the Inanoka. "I know you're a Skinwalker." She glanced at her patient. "Just like Nick."

There was a flurry of feathers as the bird grew into a woman—a beautiful woman with dark flowing hair and eyes nearly black. She was tall and lithe and lovely. She could be a cover model for native beauty, wrapped in a cloak of glossy feathers.

An instant later she stood in a fashionable dress with fitted sleeves and a modest neckline. An outer corset constructed of crisscrossing ribbons hugged her slim torso, which made the free-flowing skirt appear even more feminine. High-laced boots clung to her calves. Her hair was swept up in a sculptural bun that would have taken an ordinary woman hours to achieve. She wore no makeup and needed none. The Skinwalker was stunning.

Jessie felt a roaring fire of jealousy consume her.

The woman arched a brow as she surveyed Jessie's outfit with slow disdain. "I didn't know the circus was in town. But then, Niyanoka never did have any fashion sense."

Jessie felt the sting of the insult. Her odd combination of night clothing was made more evident by the flawless attire the Skinwalker wore.

The woman was a knockout, making Jessie feel as though she had just crawled out from under a rock.

"How do you know what I am?" asked Jessie.

"A Dream Walker, you mean? Typical for a Spirit Child to think they are the only creatures who can read auras."

This insult stung even more because it was true. She had been taught just that and Jessie could not quite keep her mouth from gaping open as she learned otherwise. It took a moment to compose herself.

"Why are you here?" she managed, keeping between Nick and this stranger.

"I picked up that Nick was in distress. I've been following him ever since."

Jessie thought of the Whirlwind. "I didn't hear a storm."

"I don't like the Thunderbirds. We had words. And the journey is a nightmare on my feathers." She lifted her arms as if to show Jessie. "So, I fly solo. It takes longer, but the experience is unparalleled."

Jessie recalled that ravens were the only creature that could fly to the Spirit World. That alone made this woman a powerful spiritual creature, but to be able to fly...

The Skinwalker strode past her and sat on the bed,

beside Nick. Jessie had an irrational impulse to shove her to the floor. Instead, she stayed close.

What was the relationship between these two?

The Skinwalker stroked his bruised cheek. "Look what they've done to you."

She glared at Jessie. The look alone was enough to cause Jessie to step back. The woman had a savageness only thinly veiled by her high-end wardrobe.

"Did you do this?"

"I found him on my property, terribly injured. I got him help."

Bess pointed to the sloppy stitches. "You call this help? You should be horsewhipped." She was on her feet, stalking Jessie as if she meant to do the job. "Why you? Why didn't he go to the Healer or to me? Are you one of his women?"

Jessie caught her breath, taken aback by the barrage of questions. Just how many women did he have?

"I never met him before."

"This makes no sense. I will take him." The woman returned to Nick's side.

Jessie took a step after her and then stopped herself from the appearance of resentment. Damned if she'd let this mortician's feather duster take Nick from her.

She quickly reined in her gut reaction and impulse for a quick refusal as she recognized that this solved her problem. Nicholas would be taken care of, she would have fulfilled her promise and she would not have to keep him in her home. Temptation would be removed.

Niyanoka thought with their minds, not their instincts, and this was the logical course.

She breathed deeply, surprised at the continued disquiet rumbling through her like distant thunder. Where was the relief that should be hers? She could not admit to this woman that she wanted him here and so took refuge in her logic.

"But they brought him to me," said Jessie.

The woman's graceful brows descended low over her dark eyes. "Who?"

"The Thunderbirds. He said he asked them to bring him to a healer and they brought him here."

The shifter rose with a suddenness that sent Jessie into retreat. "*They* brought him to you?"

The shock and incredulity made her words sharp, an accusation.

Jessie nodded.

The woman lowered her dark brows as she studied Jessie. "Then he must stay here."

Nagi had gathered thirty ghosts on the earth and began sorting who would go for judgment and who he would keep to fight in his army. A soul here or there would not be missed.

He felt the buzz of an approaching ghost, which was unusual as most fled when they sensed him. He turned and recognized one of his early enlistees.

"Lord, a raven visits the wounded wolf."

A raven? He knew her. His earlier guards had told him of a wolf and raven who visited the bear.

"Follow the raven."

"Yes, Lord."

"And don't lose her, if you value your soul."

The ghost bowed.

"Have you dealt with the Dream Walker?"

"Soon Lord, she will be gone."

Nagi rippled with satisfaction.

"Go and follow the raven. Report back when the wolf is alone."

Chapter 12

"**B**ut why?" Jessie could not keep the panic from her voice.

"The Thunderbirds can see the future. So there must be more to you than your tragic sense of fashion," said Bess.

Jessie's upset was momentarily overshadowed by her extreme dislike for this shifter. "This is a ranch. My clothing is practical, not…artifice." She pointed at the woman's stylish dress.

She fixed her dark eyes on Jessie and again Jessie felt herself being judged. At last a slight smile curled her lips. Jessie thought it made her look more dangerous.

"So you love animals?"

"Yes."

"And you are a Dream Walker?"

Jessie inclined her head.

"And you have already fallen in love with our Nicholas here."

Jessie hesitated in her rush to deny the accusation as she felt the shadow of doubt, followed by the fear, that a hasty denial would be an admission of guilt.

"Ah," said the woman, seating herself in the reading chair. "I see. Well, you're not alone. Women all over the world fall in love with him. It is as common as rain in New York."

Jessie mustered her emotions and then her denial. "Don't be silly. He's an Inanoka."

The shifter's eyes twinkled. "Oh, I see. Forbidden fruit. How delicious. I'm Bess, by the way."

"Jessie Healy."

"A pleasure." She crossed her ankles and drew back her long legs. The heels on her boots looked deadly as daggers. "And please don't be jealous. Nick and I have been on and off for decades. Like comfort food." Bess smiled, seeming to enjoy watching her words strike Jessie. "Don't look so shocked. Nick will sleep with any female who lets him. He's a wolf, after all."

Bess released her from the scrutiny of her watchful gaze and turned her attention back to Nick. Jessie felt her face heat at the look of longing the woman cast him. It was so obvious she loved Nick. Jessie resisted the urge to lift the paperweight again. She was taken aback by this new, dangerous impulse and came up short. Niyanoka did not act without thought and certainly not in anger.

Bess scrutinized her and her lips twitched. "Ah, yes, he has that effect on people. I see he still has the old magic. Managed it even without his pretty face. Impressive."

Jessie pressed her lips together, refusing to confirm or deny the woman's suspicions. She did not like the feeling of being just one in a string of this Skinwalker's conquests.

"So what will you do about it?"

"About what?" Jessie chose not to deny her jumbled emotions but instead to lay her cards on the table. "Look, I agreed to care for him as best I could. Even if I were attracted, I cannot have anything to do with him. My family would absolutely disown me if they knew I even had one under my roof."

"Two," corrected Bess.

"Exactly."

"So you won't fight for him?"

"Fight?" She shook her head. "No. There is no future for us."

Bess rose. "Well, that is true, if you are not willing to fight for him. It's what alpha females do, you know? The wolves always have an alpha. She is the only one that mates. She fights the others to earn her position and, with it, the exclusive right to the alpha male." She moved to Nick's side and stroked his neck.

Jessie balled her hands into fists and resisted the urge to plant one of them into the shifter's gut.

Bess drew her hand back from Nick's collar and stared at Jessie, challenging her with her glittering black eyes. "Any female who won't fight even her own pack for the right to take him, well, she doesn't stand a chance." Bess rose from the bed, her smile triumphant.

"So don't worry, little Spirit Child. He won't disturb the neat order of your little world for long. He'll leave you by and by."

Jessie hated the smug satisfaction in the woman's expression. But her malevolence dissolved against the realization that her words were true. When Nick left her, he would not be back.

"Ah, well," said Bess. "You'll get over him. And if not, at least your secret will be safe with me. I'll never tell."

Bess strode from the room, leaving Jessie to hurry after her. "Where are you going?"

"To Sebastian, I think. He will want to know." Bess swept past her and did not pause until she was on the front porch. Only then did Jessie see that the sky was a deep midnight blue. The stars had disappeared as the world spun from night to morning.

Bess faced Jessie. "I feel sorry for you, Niyanoka. But you lack the courage to take what you want."

Jessie did not know what to say to this.

Bess smiled. "Goodbye, Niyanoka. Perhaps it is best, for you don't deserve him. Take comfort in the knowledge that no woman before you has ever brought that one to heel. He has always been and ever will be wild."

With that she lifted her arms and transformed into a sleek black bird.

She flapped into the air and then turned, hovering at eye level.

"Keep him safe or answer to me," croaked the bird.

The raven flapped her great wings and lifted into the air, rapidly disappearing in the twilight sky.

Jessie didn't know what shocked her more, the warning or hearing it from a talking bird.

Far to the north and west, many days' travel, even as the crow flies, Michaela nestled beside her two tiny infants.

Her body ached, her head pounded and she felt thirsty and weak. Yet she had succeeded in bringing her babies into the world. Sebastian pressed a cool cloth to her forehead and she smiled up at him.

Behind him, Virginia Thistleback, the wise old Inanoka swan, bustled about in human form, removing the soiled bedding and then readying the bassinets.

She returned to Michaela's side and extended her arms. Even at nearly three hundred, the woman was strong and as hearty as an oak. Her hair was white as the feathers that covered her in her animal state, but Michaela wondered if her hair might always have been that color.

"Time for you to rest," said Thistleback.

She hesitated, not wanting to give up her babes so soon. After a fifteen-hour struggle she was exhausted, but her instinct was to keep them close.

"For pity's sake, look at your poor husband. He's half dead on his feet. Give me the babies so he can lie down."

Michaela glanced at Sebastian and noted the deep circles under his eyes. He looked dreadful.

"If you're lucky, you'll have two hours before they'll

want feeding. They're asleep. Quickly now, you sleep, too."

Michaela carefully lifted her son and firstborn into her midwife's hands.

"Careful, now," Michaela cautioned and received a scornful glance from Thistleback.

"Raised who knows how many chicks myself, and helped with the chicks orphaned by those blasted arctic foxes. He's less fragile than an egg, I'd wager." Despite her harsh words, she cradled the infant tenderly and with an experience that made Michaela slightly envious.

This was all so new to her and she worried that she would not be up to the task of mothering twins. Not just any twins, but the firstborn of the Inanoka and Niyanoka races. She was actually relieved to see they looked human, which had made Sebastian laugh. Apparently, all Inanoka were born in human form.

Thistleback returned a moment later for their daughter, scooping her up and carrying her off. "I'm putting them in the same basket for now, since they're such tiny little things."

"Thank you," murmured Michaela. She was grateful for the woman's wisdom, experience and for the gracious way she had opened her home to them at their time of need.

Skinwalkers were such kindhearted people, despite their fierceness and violent reputations. Her people were so wrong about them.

Sebastian crawled in beside her, and she inched over, feeling the muscles of her legs and the sensitive tissues inside her all cry out in protest.

"When they wake up, send the bear for them. Never too soon to get accustomed to holding them. And you—" she pointed at Michaela "—are to stay in bed, unless you need to use the privy. Understand?"

Michaela nodded.

"Call if you need me. Like all swans, I sleep lightly." She clicked the door behind her, leaving them alone for the first time since before the contractions began.

Michaela turned to find Sebastian propped up on one elbow, gazing down at her with a look of adoration that made her heart catch in her chest.

"How do you feel?" he asked.

As if she'd just birthed a camel—with two humps— was what she wanted to say, but he seemed so excited and exhausted and caring. She thought him just dear.

Funny, for he was a massive man and a formidable grizzly bear when in animal form. He could make man or beast turn tail and run just by rearing on his hind legs.

But to her, he was everything, so she lied.

"I feel wonderful."

He rested a hand on her arm and squeezed her tenderly. "You did well, little mother."

She smiled at that, exhaustion taking hold. She lifted her chin and he kissed her on the lips.

"Do you think they will be Seers?" she asked.

Sebastian gazed into his wife's lovely worried eyes and answered the question she was really asking. If they were Seers like their mother, then Nagi would want them dead.

"I'll keep them safe, love. I'll protect them and you, even from him."

She smiled and nestled against him, confident in her husband, but it was a long time before sleep found Sebastian. He believed his wife's dream. Nick had been attacked. He worried about his friend. He wanted to go to him and heal his injuries. But to do so meant leaving his family unprotected. His instincts warred with his loyalty.

The Ruler of the Circle of Ghosts wanted his wife and children dead. And now he was attacking his friends to get to them.

For the first time in his life, Sebastian felt powerless.

Chapter 13

Jessie spent the remainder of the night sleeping in the chair beside Nick. She did not dare leave him alone after the strange appearance of the raven.

She slept fitfully, waking at last with relief to see that dawn had cast the sky in pale pink.

She stood and tried unsuccessfully to roll the kink out of her neck before creeping to Nick's bed. She rested a hand on his forehead, troubled by the warmth that told her he had a low fever, but more troubled by the fact that he did not stir. She had not been able to get near him yesterday without him rousing.

This change troubled her deeply.

He needed the antibiotics. She left his side to retrieve them, determined to quickly throw some hay to the horses and then return to her patient.

She was halfway across the room when she recalled

the details of her conversation with last night's visitor. If she didn't know better, she'd say it was a bad dream. Much of what had happened to her lately fell into that category. But a Dream Walker always knew reality from the creations of the mind. The raven could not be dismissed as some vision. She had been here and had so much as told her that she and Nicholas were lovers, then made a crack about Jessie lacking courage.

"Well, why should I care *what* she said?" she muttered.

But she did. The magnitude by which she did care rattled her as much as the realization that the raven was correct: she was wildly attracted to Nick.

"But that's not love. It's lust." She flicked on the kitchen light and stooped to tug on her high rubber boots. "I'm not made of stone. He's attractive, available. It's only natural."

Jessie was not a prude. In her early adulthood, she had taken a variety of human lovers, which was relatively common for her kind. She had tried and failed to meet a fellow Niyanoka who was willing to live in so isolated a place. Most of her people preferred cities or larger urban centers than the country road she currently called home. But no one she knew had ever even spoken to a Skinwalker. There was no question that she tread upon extremely dangerous ground.

Before she reached the front door, her cell phone, which sat on the counter, began to vibrate and flash. She lifted the thing, forcing her eyes open enough to read the display: Larry Karr.

Her neighbor, who could see her kitchen windows

from his upstairs. She sighed and flipped open the phone.

"Hi, Larry."

"Saw your light. How's the wolf."

"Fine. No problems," she lied.

"Need any help with him?"

The thoughtfulness of her neighbors, which had always reinforced her belief in the goodness of humanity had suddenly become a real pain in the ass.

"I got him out in the barn."

She heard him chuckle.

"Bet the horses love that."

"Just for a few days. Then I'll let him go."

"Thought you said he was a pet."

"Yeah, let him go back to his owners, I mean. They're coming to get him. I'm petsitting."

"Jessie, you really okay?"

"Sure, Larry."

"My nephew works for the ambulance corp. He said they found an injured man on your property after that storm. Said he refused treatment."

"That's right. His wife came and got him. No insurance, you see."

"Ah. Well, you had a busy day."

"Thanks for checking, Larry. Give my best to May and the girls."

"Okay, I…"

Jessie closed the phone, turned it off and placed it back on the counter, then headed out the door. She paused on the steps, as she always did, to glance out of the window at the pasture across the road.

It was her custom to see what her mares were doing. At this hour, they usually lined the fence, staring hopefully at the house in preparation for her arrival with breakfast hay. But today they stood herded together at the far corner of the pasture, tossing their heads with restless glances toward the barn.

Jessie wrinkled her brow and turned in the direction of their nervous glances.

Her grip on the doorknob slackened and she leaned forward in her double take.

There, beside her barbed-wire fence, grazed a massive male buffalo. "Oh, what now?"

She headed for the gun closet and retrieved a high-power rifle, then loaded it, recalling that last night she'd nearly used the same bullets on Nicholas Chien.

She left the house with the intention of getting her mares into the barn before calling the national park to see if they were missing a bull.

But buffalo didn't generally just wander away from the herd. Maybe it was a sick animal or a young bull chased off by a stronger male. She crept off the porch, eyeing it critically. The beast looked healthy, strong, as big as a minivan and about as bright.

Jessie inched forward slowly, edging behind her truck, and then hesitated. She'd have to cross the road, without cover.

The buffalo lifted his head and seemed to be staring directly at her.

She ducked behind her truck, clutching her rifle before her as she pointed the barrel toward the brightening sky. A moment later she heard hooves striking the pavement.

"Son of a..." She peeked over the flatbed to see the monster making a beeline for her. "Bitch!"

She raised the rifle, using the truck bed to steady her aim. The buffalo stopped. She stared down the sight, lining up the bead and notch just behind the creature's shoulder blade. But the dust surrounding the thick hide obscured her shot. The dust hung about the bull a good ten inches above its hump. She squinted in the first rays of sunlight as another possibility occurred to her.

Auras were hard to see at the best of times, but at sunrise they were nearly impossible to spot. Still, that did look like an aura.

She lifted her head and lowered the rifle. She could still take her shot, but it wouldn't hurt to check.

Jessie drew a breath and lifted her chin.

"Are you here to see Nicholas?"

The bull pawed at the blacktop. Why didn't one of those semis show up when she needed it?

She felt silly shouting at a buffalo. "The Skinwalker? He's inside."

The buffalo turned from her and headed toward her house. She ran behind the truck, shouting as she went.

"Wait. You can't go in there like that. Please change forms first."

The bull swung its massive head in her direction, causing her to stagger back. There was a puff of dust as the male transformed into a young Native American, wrapped in a buffalo robe. An instant later, he stood in worn jeans, dusty work boots and a fringed leather shirt that made him look like some kind of reenactor at the annual rendezvous. He beat at his shirt, raising a cloud of dust.

Jessie prayed to the Great Spirit that her neighbor was not still standing in his upstairs window. "Been a while since I walked as a man," he said by way of apology. "How did you know?"

She flipped the safety to the on position. "I'm Jessie."

"Tuff," he said and lifted a foot to rest on the first step of her stairs. "Tuff Jackson. Actually Jackson is just where I come from. Don't know my real surname. Long story."

"Can I help you?"

"I'm here to help him." He thumbed toward the door. "Heard his call for help."

"Do you know him?"

The man wore his thick black hair in traditional twin braids, secured with leather sheaths made of short brown fur.

"Never had the pleasure. I can tell from the scent he's a wolf. Don't hang around wolves as a rule."

She and Tuff exchanged a smile.

"Understandable."

He paused, pointed a thumb at her kitchen door. "Your place?"

"Yeah." She rounded the truck and offered her hand, shocked at herself for welcoming him. "Thanks for coming."

She headed up the steps and held the door open. He stepped past her. She thought a buffalo shifter would be big and burly, like a professional wrestler. But this man was slight and young, seeming only in his early teens. Of course, he could be eighty for all she knew. Inanoka lived even longer than her people.

The buffalo man paused in her kitchen, looking around. "Nice place." He focused on her now. "How'd you know what I was?"

"I'm a Spirit Child."

His eyes rounded. "Ah. Never met one before." He looked her over. "What's your gift?"

"I'm a Dream Walker."

"Have you tried healing him in his sleep?"

She flushed at the reminder of what she had done. "Not exactly."

"You could, you know. Just the suggestion would at the very least greatly ease his pain."

"I've never done that. I deal mainly with injuries to the mind."

"But your power is greater than that."

"How do you know?"

"I can sense power, energy flows. Yours is great. But in the meantime, I'll try."

Jessie took a long look at Tuff. Now inside, his aura became clearer. Healers usually had a deep blue energy to them. His seemed more the color of rust. She paused before leading him to her patient, feeling protective of Nick. "Are you a Healer?"

"Not exactly."

She felt off balance and unsure of allowing a stranger near Nick. Jessie could not understand why she hesitated. She should be happy to have another Skinwalker offer assistance. Perhaps he could release her from her promise and spare them both from this strange attraction.

But until that happened, she had promised to see him well and would see it through.

"How do you pick up his call?"

"It's a disturbance, like a dust storm, but inside your mind. You have to concentrate to get the direction and then you just follow it. It can travel a few hundred miles, unless you know each other, then, I don't know, farther, I think."

Nick had told her he had no one, yet here was another who could help. Who else had he called?

Tuff inclined his head toward Nick's room, silently asking entrance.

She drew a breath to gather her resolve, putting the rifle on the counter, and then led the way. She paused just inside the doorway of her study, gazing at Nicholas and checking his steady, even draw of breath. The sight reassured her. He still rested comfortably. When he was awake, his breathing was shallow and his face strained. He had slept long into the morning. She glanced at the open bottle of painkillers beside his bed. How many had he taken?

She took a step toward him, but Tuff passed her, drawing up a chair beside him.

"What are his injuries?"

She told him.

"What happened to him?"

She sighed, sat on the corner of the desk and began the telling. His eyes widened at her mention of the three ghosts and he looked perplexed when she told of the couple Nick said he protected.

"And you say this couple, they are an Inanoka and Niyanoka?"

She nodded. "That is what I have been told."

"The world is full of wonders. I do not think it is impossible."

Tuff looked down at Nicholas. He didn't look tough, not in the form of a man at least. He didn't seem insightful like Bess or charming like Nick. He just seemed serious as he stared at Nicholas.

She knew buffalo were sacred, that the Great Mystery had brought buffalo to man so they would have all they needed to live. They were selfless creatures to submit to death so the people might live. Animals of sacrifice.

But she wondered what held he could give do Nick. Perhaps he would act as a watchdog, protecting him from future attacks while he healed.

Certainly he would be a formidable opponent in animal form.

Nicholas could track anyone anywhere just by their scent. According to Nicholas, his friend the grizzly could heal any natural injury. What was the raven's power? Something to do with the Spirit World, she'd guess. Could she see the future? And what were the powers of the buffalo?

Her musing had taken her mind far afield and so she had not noticed that Tuff was chanting a prayer. She sat quietly until he finished.

"Could you get me some water, please?"

"I have coffee."

"No, just water. A tall glass, please."

She left him for the time it took to fill her largest glass. When she reentered the room, she found the man kneeling with his hands stretched toward the ceiling, praying again. His shirt, shoes and belt were gone, leaving him dressed only in his jeans. His body was narrow, hairless and slim. If she were to pick an animal he most resembled, she might say a weasel or coyote. She stared at the hollow beneath his ribs. About his neck hung a single buffalo tooth, wrapped in a band of colorful seed beads fashioned to resemble the hoof prints of a buffalo in white on a green background. The leather cord had several larger beads evenly spaced along the necklace. It thumped rhythmically against his chest as he rocked forward and backward with his prayer.

He ended with a sharp cry that made Jessie's blood curdle. She found herself choking the water glass.

Tuff smiled at her. "Thank you."

He rose to take the water and drank it down as if he was parched. Then he kneeled beside Nicholas.

Only then did she realize he had uncovered Nick, drawing the blankets, folding them carefully over his feet. Most peculiar of all was that he had torn away the bandages on his eye and at his chest, revealing the hole where the chest tube had been.

"Hey, he needs those."

Tuff lifted a hand toward her. "Hush now."

He rested one palm on Nicholas's forehead and the other on the middle of his belly. He closed his eyes.

Jessie felt a disturbance in the air, as if a breeze blew

through the bedroom, except the trees outside were still. The indoor disturbance spun in circles, lifting loose papers on her desk.

She was so distracted by the strange wind that pricked at her skin like static electricity that she did not notice Tuff. His face was now beaded with sweat and the muscles at his cheeks bulged. He was pale and every line of his young face showed strain.

This was like no healing ceremony she had ever witnessed. Something dangerous passed between these two, something dark. She sensed it in the dimming of Tuff's aura and the startling crackling in the air.

She moved to flee but instead found herself at the foot of the daybed, standing like a sentinel. She did not know of what use she might be, but she would intervene if Nicholas showed signs of distress.

She stared at Nick's face and had to blink to be sure of her own eyes. The scabs on his cheek, forehead and eyelids dropped away like gorged ticks. She gasped and looked to Tuff for some explanation. Instead, she had to force her hand to her mouth to keep from crying out. The familiar gouges now marred Tuff's flesh.

Chapter 14

Tuff's face swelled as the deep red marks grew longer and gaped open. Blood streamed down his cheek and neck, but he kept his hands on Nicholas.

What was this? She backed away and then halted. She wanted to run, but she could not abandon Nick. Stronger even than her instinct for self-preservation was her need to protect him. She glanced from one Skinwalker to the other. Nick's breathing grew rapid and Tuff's shallow.

Jessie's jaw ached from clenching as she watched the deep blue-and-red bruises bloom on Tuff's previously unmarred ribs. She heard a loud crack.

Tuff hissed and leaned toward the injury, bracing against the pain as he struggled to hold his position. Jessie was certain that beneath his smooth young skin, his ribs were breaking.

"Stop," she called to him. "Stop now."

She grasped his shoulder to pull him away, but the electric shock of pain threw her backward. She landed hard on her backside, feeling as if he had punched her in the chest. Her ribs ached, but Tuff had not moved.

She rose unsteadily but did not try to intervene again. Instead, she stood with her hands clasped and pressed to her open mouth. Her front teeth bit into the flesh of her index finger as she stared in mute horror.

Finally, Tuff's hands slipped from Nick's head and belly and he collapsed to the floor.

"Tuff," she cried and rushed to him, but paused before touching him again. He was cold and his hair damp from sweat. Blood matted his long braids. "Oh, what did you do to yourself?"

Tears ran down her cheeks as she gazed down at the boy. He had taken Nicholas's pain. She was in awe of the selfless powers this Skinwalker possessed. This was not a power given to heartless killers, for such a selfless gift would be useless among such a race. No, the Great Spirit would grant such a power only to those who understood selflessness and sacrifice. Jessie stared down in wonder as she realized she had discovered a deep respect for their kind.

Tuff's face bled crimson rivers. She knelt beside him.

"Stay back," said Tuff.

She didn't want to, but she did as he asked. Would he bear the scars on his face for the rest of his life? They were not his to bear. She was grateful, but so sad. It wasn't fair.

Then she noticed something. She inched closer, not

sure she should believe her eyes. Yet, it seemed as if the cuts were growing shallower.

"You're healing!"

Tuff's face now held pink streaks where the gashes had been only an instant before. He straightened, as if his ribs were knitting beneath his skin. The bruising dissolved away by slow measures, changing before her eyes.

"How do you do that?"

Tuff's pale face showed strain and his eyes were somber reflections of concern. "It's not finished. His body is whole now, but his mind is beyond my reach."

Jessie glanced at Nick, seeing how still he lay, his breathing barely moving his bare ribs.

She turned to Tuff. "What do you mean?"

Jessie knelt at Nick's bedside, staring down at the dark feathery lashes that brushed his pale cheeks. It was the face she had seen in his dream, but not his face, for here his cheeks held no glow and his skin was as bloodless as stone. "I don't understand."

Tuff hugged his ribs and struggled to a sitting position on the floor. "His mind is resting far away and I have no talent to reach him. My gift is purely corporal."

Jessie felt her panic rise to her throat, squeezing off her air, as she turned to Nick. She grasped his wrist, feeling for a pulse. *Thready, weak,* reported the analytical portion of her mind.

"Nick!" She tapped his smooth cheek and got no response. "What's happening?"

"He cannot hear you now."

"A coma, are you talking about a coma?"

"Yes."

"But it doesn't make sense. He was getting better. What did you do to him?"

Tuff shook his head. "I did nothing but heal. It is a mystery to me."

Desperation choked her. "I promised him I'd take care of him."

"Then you must. Hurry, Dream Walker, for he is sliding from this world."

"What do you want me to do?"

"Follow him. Reach into his mind and convince him he has not finished walking this path."

"But I have never… I mean, I only enter dreams. He's not sleeping."

"No, he is dying."

The panic pounded with her frantic heart. "Even if I could, I can't just project. I have to be calm and relaxed, meditating."

Tuff gave her a worried look. "You must do what must be done. I will sit with you and pray while you use your gift."

He dragged a chair beside the bed and offered it to her. She glanced at Tuff, who sat peacefully in her reading chair, as if Nick were not dying before them.

Jessie sat, drew a deep breath and closed her eyes. But all she could think of was that she believed Nick. He had to live to protect the Healer and the Seer. He was needed here. Her panic choked her ability to relax. It took many tries and false starts before she finally sank into her meditative state and felt the click of disengagement as her astral body separated from her physical one, reaching out to find Nick in the void.

This dream was different than any of Jessie's experiences. It did not reflect color and life, but was a dead predawn gray, a shadow land of dark, menacing outlines.

"I saw them."

She startled at his voice, so near yet she could not see him.

"Nick, you must wake up now."

"I heard them talking. There are two of them now. They're watching."

She felt a prickle run like rodents' feet up her spine. "Who?"

"Ghosts. Nagi sent them. If I go to the Healer, they will follow. If I don't go, they will hurt you. How could they know?"

The melancholy of his vision chilled her nearly as much as the hopelessness of his tone.

"Know what?"

"That if they hurt you badly enough, I would jeopardize everything to save you."

Her eyes adjusted by slow degrees. She could make him out now as he stood, head down.

"Nick, you must come back."

He lifted his head. "I'm sorry I dragged you into the middle of this. I had no right."

What could she say to convince him. "Nick, I trust you to protect me."

"If I were whole, that would be true. But as I am, I am useless as your protector."

"But you're healed. The buffalo fixed everything."

"What?" Nick stepped closer and she could see his muscular form.

"You are whole and strong. You *can* protect me and together we can find a way to warn the Seer."

Nick reached for her, then hesitated. "Together?"

She gazed up at him quizzically. "Of course."

He stared at her, but something in his eyes was so sad.

"What is it?" she asked.

"It's just, I never…I never felt this protective of another person. It weakens me. It gives my enemy a tool to use in the destruction of my friend."

"Caring for others is what strengthens us."

He stepped closer. "You're wrong. It was my father's love for me that brought him to an ambush."

"No, it was your mother's betrayal. Not your doing."

"Perhaps. But such connections are liabilities I cannot afford."

Connections? Did he care for her? The idea excited her for a moment and then she felt a nervous flutter in her belly. In that moment she knew what he meant. Liabilities, complications, a relationship with this man would be all of that and more. The notion of caring for a Skinwalker scared her out of her wits. And she didn't understand the attraction they shared. It was like nothing in her experience. It wasn't caring. It could not be love. They just met. Love did not work that way; it required time, commitment.

In any case, she must first bring him from this shadow land.

He moved as close as he could without touching her. "Do you feel anything for me?"

She wanted to deny it but hesitated, somehow knowing intuitively that his return depended upon her answer. She lifted her chin and met his pale eyes. The safest path for her was to reject this strange attraction that tugged at her even now. But to protect Nick, she must expose herself in the most raw way possible by admitting to something that she was forbidden to feel.

"Jessie?" He extended his hand.

"Nick, come back to me."

The touch electrified her with a rippling energy. At the contact, she sensed the depth of his protective instinct for her and it stunned her.

His eyes glowed pale gray as they rounded in astonishment, as if he read something from their touch as well. "Together, then."

He squeezed her hand and the gray world brightened to a flash of brilliant gold. She blinked her eyes and found herself sitting at his bedside.

Tuff sat quietly across the room, a placid smile upon his lips.

"What happened?" she asked.

"You asked him to come back to you and you touched his hand. After that his breathing changed." Tuff motioned to Nick. "Look."

Nick's eyes blinked open and he stared at her in astonishment. She knew that she had lost her mask of aloof indifference. He would recall every word of their meeting. She held her breath as he studied her face.

She grinned at him, happy to have him back. He

returned her smile and her heartbeat jumped like a young colt. How could she have guessed that the torn and swollen face could transform into such perfection? His smooth, strong jaw begged her to stroke it. She wanted to explore the hollows beneath his cheeks and touch the dark feathery lashes that framed his frosty blue eyes. His full lips made her remember their dream encounter.

"You're even handsomer than in your dream."

He chuckled. From behind them, Tuff cleared his throat and stood stiffly.

"Welcome back."

Nick's attention flicked to Tuff as he leaped off the bed with such speed and agility, Jessie gasped. Nick landed in a crouch, placing himself between Jessie and the other male.

"Who are you?" Nick growled.

"His name is Tuff."

Nick inhaled. "A buffalo." His voice held a note of wonder and his shoulders relaxed.

"Will you look at him!" said Tuff, his voice ringing with pride and excitement.

Nick seemed completely recovered. His jaw dropped open as the realization sunk in. He clapped both hands on his torso and drew a deep breath.

Jessie glanced at Tuff, but the man did not share her smile. He swayed on his feet, still sweating and pale.

"He still feels it," she whispered, stepping closer.

"Yes." Nick stooped beside him and Jessie followed. Nick studied the young man. "Can I do anything?"

She stared at Tuff's ribs. The purple-and-blue bruises

faded to green, then brown. At last there was nothing but a large patch of red skin.

"I am nearly whole again. I need only a short rest." He sank wearily back into the chair and closed his eyes. His breathing changed almost instantly.

"Tuff?" she said, and when she received no answer, she glanced at Nick.

"A trance. He will be all right in a little while."

"That's miraculous. He healed you."

"No, not healed. Buffalo have great strength, but they cannot heal. They can only assume the injuries of others."

She met his troubled gaze. "He broke his bones for you—a stranger."

"Buffalo must be strong and noble to do such things."

"But what if you were paralyzed? What if you had cancer? Could he still do this?"

"I don't know. Every creature, even the mighty ones, has limits. They can't raise the dead. That much I know." He rubbed his neck. "Well, maybe they can, but it kills them."

"How do you know that?"

"All Inanoka hear the tales of the buffalo. They are legendary." He kneeled beside the chair and laid a hand on the buffalo, then quickly drew it back. "His ribs are still healing."

Tuff's eyes flickered open. He stared up at Nick and smiled, seemingly satisfied with his accomplishment.

"Thank you, brother," said Nick.

"Walk in beauty," replied Tuff.

Jessie recognized the blessing and felt a lump in her throat. He had taken Nick's pain and then blessed him. Her admiration for Inanoka grew.

Every single thing she had learned about these Skinwalkers was wrong. Her mother called them talking animals, one of the few names she could repeat without blushing.

How could her people hate such nobility?

It was then she realized how closely she stood to Nicholas. She tilted her head to gaze up at his restored face. He was as he had been in the dream, powerful, devilishly handsome and staring at her with a longing that made her skin flush in anticipation.

His nostrils flared as he inhaled and then smiled. She recalled his acute sense of smell and wondered if he could detect her desire. His knowing smile removed all doubt.

Nick inclined his head toward Tuff. "I think we'd better see to him first."

This reminder and his assumption that she would act on her impulses irritated her. Her face went from warm to hot as she felt her emotions churn. This also was unlike a Niyanoka, who prided themselves on control of animal impulses.

"I am not in the habit of doing whatever comes into my head."

"Too bad. I'm sure you'd enjoy it."

She resisted the urge to slap his smooth cheek. Jessie whirled toward the kitchen on the pretext of getting her new patient some water. When she returned, Nick was sitting in the office chair beside Tuff and the two were speaking in low tones.

Nick noticed her first, probably well before she even entered the room. It was maddening the way he could track her by scent and by sound.

She glared at Nick and then gave Tuff a warm smile. "That was very brave." Jessie managed to get the pitcher and glass on the side table without touching Nick. "Are you thirsty?"

Tuff nodded. A moment later she offered him a full glass.

"How long until you are healed?"

"Oh, very soon. Only one of the ribs was bad. The other two were just cracked."

Nick winced.

Tuff tried to laugh and then began coughing. The water helped. Jessie sat on the bed and rested a hand on his, feeling the tingling ache begin in her ribs. He patted her hand and then set it away, as if he was trying to comfort and protect her, as well.

"Don't worry," he said.

But of course she did. Of the two, Tuff was the gentle one, the thoughtful one. So why did she feel nothing when she touched him? It was Nick she was aware of, every move, every glance. He didn't have to touch her to be disturbing. She did not realize she was gazing at Nicholas until Tuff's bemused voice interjected.

"You two want me to crawl outside?"

Jessie forced her attention back to Tuff. "You're mistaken. There's nothing between us."

Tuff glanced at Nick, who winked.

"She keeps telling herself that."

Tuff smiled at Jessie. "I do not like to disagree with my hostess, but there *is* something between you."

"You misunderstand," she insisted.

"I can feel the tug between you." He held her gaze. "And your resistance, but this is not within your control. I do not understand this pair bond. It is unlike a female in heat. Nor is it like the lust of humans. I only know that you call to him and he answers."

Jessie stood. "That's absurd. I'm not calling anyone."

Nick leaned close to Tuff. "Stubborn."

Tuff did not share Nick's cavalier smile. "Careful, brother. Something is happening here. Something new. The Thunderbirds forecast it, or they would not have left you here. This woman is more to you than her resistance. More than a new challenge."

Nick stopped smiling and he stood. Jessie noted the worry on his face. The expression did not suit him. He was always so confident. But now she went cold at the uncertainty reflected in his ice-blue eyes.

Chapter 15

Nagi received the messenger as he took his next woman with the body of a host. The undulating rhythm was somewhat distracting but he focused on the ghost.

"What?" he snapped.

"Lord, a buffalo Skinwalker has restored the wolf's body."

"What!" Nagi's concentration snapped and he slipped from the human host with such jarring force he damaged the human's brain. Beneath him the woman tried to rouse her husband, but he lay unconscious upon her.

Nagi turned to his ghost hovering beside him.

"Forgive me, Lord."

Nagi had no time for groveling. "Have they left the Dream Walker?"

"The buffalo is preparing to do so."

"What of the wolf?"

"I do not know. He has not spoken of it, Lord."

Why hadn't the wolf left? It would have been the first thing Nagi would have done in hopes of escaping his pursuers.

"Has the Dream Walker left them?"

"She has not, Lord."

She?

"The Dream Walker is female?"

"Yes, Lord."

New possibilities arose. He now understood why a Dream Walker might help a wolf and why he did not flee the instant he was well. Could these two be mates?

"Attack the Dream Walker, but do not kill her. Report back if the wolf defends her."

"Yes, Lord."

If he was right, the Dream Walker was the key. But were the wolf's feelings for this female strong enough that he would reveal the Healer to save her?

Tuff was well enough to sit at her kitchen table for supper. He was a vegetarian, so she cooked pasta with sauce, garlic bread and a fine green salad. Throughout the meal Jessie thought of Nick's dream and his contact with the ghosts. Did he really see them in his sleep?

Was she in danger?

After the meal, Tuff rose to take his leave and Jessie thanked him again. She kissed his smooth cheek and wished him a safe journey.

He and Nick thumped each other roughly on the back in the way of men.

"I owe you a great debt," said Nick.

"Just see you do not nip my heels when the snows pin me down."

Nick laughed. "I promise. I will never hunt buffalo again."

Tuff laughed. "Liar. But perhaps you will remember the old blessings when you do."

Nick nodded. "Yes, brother. This I will do."

"And I will stay close, in case you have further need of me."

Although his offer was generous, the notion that they would need his gift again chilled Jessie to the core. She hugged herself as they walked with him as far as the pasture across the road. There Tuff walked behind the barn. A buffalo emerged on the other side and continued into the wooded glen, splashed through the stream and straight up the incline beyond.

Nick and Jessie trailed slowly behind him, pausing by the stream as the buffalo turned back and tossed his massive head in farewell, then disappeared over the hilltop.

For some reason, she felt like a couple sending off an old friend. But that was silly.

Nick turned to Jessie, his eyes gleaming unnaturally bright. He was a vision of male power. Just looking at his restored face made her knees liquefy.

"Your life would have been simpler if you had not called me back."

She suddenly found the exposed earth at her feet especially fascinating.

His voice was velvet. "Why did you?"

She could not look at him. To do so would let him

see the truth, that she cared for him much more than she should.

"I wanted to protect the Seer. She's one of mine, you know."

His voice held dry amusement. "So, you believe me now?"

"Yes."

"Is the Seer the only reason?"

She glanced up into his inscrutable eyes, wishing she could tell what he was thinking. She felt so lost and confused by him. She prayed he would not use her words to mock her as she opened her heart the tiniest bit.

"This connection between us frightens me. But I believe the Thunderbirds brought you here for a reason. I want to know what that is." She swallowed her trepidation. "I didn't ask to be a part of this. But I am a part. I feel it."

"Do you? And what about the ghosts?"

She hated ghosts. She found the thought that they might be lurking about both terrifying and repugnant. She put on a brave face.

"Not all ghosts are evil."

His expression was grim. "These are."

Her stomach clenched as she recalled Nick's injuries.

"I never should have come."

He glanced after Tuff. Nick was well now. He could return to his path. All she had to do was let him walk away. Jessie pushed down the urge to cry.

Perhaps she had served her role in seeing him well. Was that all the Thunderbirds had foreseen?

She had succeeded in keeping her hands off him,

except for the disaster in his dream. If he left now, her life could return to normal. Couldn't it?

A wave of precognition shook her as she recognized she was too changed to ever go back to her old life. Her community, their beliefs, all seemed wrong to her now. But where did she belong if not with her people? He had changed her irrevocably and now he would leave her.

She had no doubt that he would go. He had made it clear that he never stayed anywhere long, nor did he have the faith required to have a relationship. What had he called his feelings for her—a liability? She did not delude herself that he would change his ways for her. She had to decide only whether she would reveal her longing for him or keep it locked forever in her heart.

Regret clenched her stomach until in ached. How bleak her life now seemed.

She didn't want him to go. "I'll miss you."

His smile was cautious and still it made her heart rate triple. "Will you? What changed your mind?"

She glanced about, as if the answer to his question might be found in the lazy flow of water in the stream or the thick grass that lined the bank. She brought her attention back to him. "You're not what I expected."

He grinned at that. "You're such a flatterer."

Her shoulders sagged. "I don't know what to do now. This isn't a dream."

"No."

She drew in a heavy breath. "I'm not like you, free to do whatever I choose. I've always been a part of a community. And I believe that love and commitment are blessings, not a curse. We are so different."

"Not so different."

He glanced to the hillside and she felt him slipping away. She steeled herself for his leaving. Any moment he would change to his animal form and disappear from her life, but not from her memory. No, she knew this man was one she would never forget.

All she could do was to keep her dignity during this goodbye. As she stared up at him, the impulse to beg him to stay tore at her. She wanted him to make love to her, again, only this time here in the real world.

Don't do something you'll regret.

Jessie sighed, knowing that whether she slept with him or not, she would face regret. The only question was, which would she regret more, taking this chance or not taking it?

She reached for him but let her hand fall back to her side. "Nick?"

He lifted his eyebrows in question.

She knew she shouldn't say it, but she was so weary of always keeping her emotions in check. She was no longer that reasonable, rational person. Somewhere in a matter of days she had lost the faithful little Spirit Child she had always been. So what was she now?

She had already admitted she had feelings for him in his dreams, when she thought he would not remember, but now she wanted to say it out loud.

She stared at the face she had grown to love. Great Mystery, she thought, she would miss that face. She wouldn't see him in the pink light of morning or on a quiet autumn evening when the cool wind blew through his hair.

No, you don't, girl. You are not falling in love with a Skinwalker. But what if she already had?

She thought of Tuff's words about a connection he did not understand and how she was more than her resistance. Then she remembered the raven's challenge that she would lose Nick because she didn't have the courage to fight for him.

She stood there before him, terrified to speak and terrified not to.

What if she overcame her resistance and found the courage to speak and he still rejected her?

Chapter 16

Nick had seen that look on a hundred female faces. He knew instinctively what came next and had a thousand clever ways to say goodbye. The difference was that this time he wanted to stay but couldn't.

Nick's unease grew as he watched Jessie struggling to speak. He smelled her agitation, a tangy combination of perspiration and uncertainty. She had lowered her defenses to love him in his dream, she had healed him with her gift and now she was poised to make the biggest mistake of her life.

He knew what loving him would cost her. But here she stood, toe-to-toe, clearing her throat and gazing up at him with eyes that offered everything. In that moment, he longed to take what she was about to offer, to end his transient life.

He had always been so careful to guard against

attachments, not wanting to give anyone, especially a woman, that kind of power over him. Now he saw he already had.

In other circumstances they might have had a chance. If she were not of a race that hated his kind and if loving her did not endanger her life.

He did not forget the ghosts or their plotting. He had heard them in his dark vision. They were going to hurt Jessie. Attack her, they had said, to separate him from his only ally. But he knew the more dangerous truth: that his feelings for Jessie not only put her in danger, but they also threatened the Healer. For Jessie's sake, he would reveal his best friend's location.

His enemies must never learn he cared, or they would use her as surely as his mother had used him.

And that was why he must make her believe she meant nothing to him. It was the only way to protect her from Nagi.

She gazed up at him with such longing. He hated himself already. She had loved him in his dreams, had called him back from the brink of eternity. And as payment, he would cut her in the cruelest way possible.

"Nick, I have to tell you something."

He clenched his jaw, gathering the courage to do what must be done.

"Yeah, me, too. You were right about the dream."

"What?"

"Nothing really happened. How could it? You're not my type. But thanks for dragging me off your lawn and for not killing me like you wanted to."

Confusion filled her eyes. "Nick, I don't understand. I thought—"

He cut her off. "Just like the rest of them. No, darling. Sorry to disappoint you. I don't sleep with the enemy. You were right about everything. My dad and I aren't so different, after all. Humans are like locusts and the planet is better off without them."

She wrinkled her brow and then blinked up at him. "But what about the Seer?"

"What about her? She's one of yours. Why should I care what happens to her?"

She opened her mouth and then closed it. Her eyes glittered with tears. "What about our connection?" she whispered.

"Connection?" He snorted, hating himself. "The only connection we have is the kind I get with every female I meet. But in this case I gotta pass."

She gasped and faltered, as if he had struck her. He reached for her but stopped himself, lifting his hand in a dismissive salute.

"Thanks for everything, Doc." He turned to go, thinking he would be haunted forever by her heartrending, grief-stricken face.

"Nick?"

Keep walking. But he paused, allowing her to catch up. She stared up at him with eyes luminous with tears and lifted her hand. He leaned away, but not far enough. She stroked his cheek and his world came crashing down. Heat and pain and desire roared through him with such force it caught his breath.

His eyes widened as she parted her lips.

He dragged her into his arms with a roughness unlike him. He was always gentle with his women, respectful and generous. But something about Jessie made him feel as if he was starving and only she could satisfy him.

Every noble thought and reasonable argument fled like a herd of elk before a pack of wolves.

His mouth slanted over hers and she opened for him. His tongue slid forward, mating with hers. The taste of her was honey.

Still this was not close enough. He placed his hand at the center of her back and flexed his arm, bringing her breasts flush against him. His other hand threaded into her thick hair, angling her head so he could devour her mouth.

The moan of pleasure that escaped her made him painfully hard. She rolled her hips toward him, sliding one knee between his thighs.

He took her backward to the earth with the swiftness of a hunter bringing down his prey. Her lips were fire, scalding the skin of his face and throat. She writhed her hips in an invitation he could not resist. He was so overwhelmed by his own need for her that it took a moment to recognize what he was feeling.

His breath caught in his throat and he stilled. She continued kissing her way down his neck as he held her, unable to believe what he was experiencing.

He had heard tell of this in legend. But until Sebastian described it, Nick thought it only that. But now he knew it existed and not just in the abstract, oh no. It existed here, now, for him, the connection that came only with one's *soul mate*.

Nick rolled her beneath him and arched back, pinning her hips to the ground while gazing down at her. Yes, he could feel everything. Every wonderful thing she felt, her burning desire, her need, and her liquid readiness for their joining.

Did she experience his desire as well? Could she sense his thoughts?

"Jessie?"

"Not now, Nick. Please don't talk now."

She opened her thighs and wrapped her long legs around him, pulling him toward her, joining them at their sex.

He rose to a kneeling position, lifting her to drag away her shirt and unfasten her bra. She slipped out of her boots and unzipped her jeans, wriggling out of them before tossing them aside. When she stretched out before him on the grass, only a pink scrap of lace caressed her hips.

Now that he was not touching her, he felt the difference. He was still half mad with his own desire, but he no longer sensed hers. He touched his necklace and all garments disappeared, their energy now contained only by the choker about his throat.

She purred. "I like that trick."

Jessie reached out and laid a possessive hand on the center of his chest. Instantly, he was consumed by her need. He pressed her back to the grass with his body.

His warm flesh melded with hers in the exquisite and torturous contact that could never be close enough. Her fingernails raked his back, causing him to arch in pleasure. She wanted him to kiss her everywhere.

He smiled at the specifics of the instructions as if he heard her speaking, yet all about them were only the calls of birds and the drone of the bees.

Nick followed her directions to her lovely plump breasts, kissing and suckling as she moaned her delight. She could not keep still beneath him now, for her longing burned too bright.

She lifted her hips and he took the opportunity to slip the sheath of lace away, removing the last barrier between them.

Her mind cried out for him. He did not need her mental urging to know what she craved, for she grasped his hips and pressed herself wantonly against his sex.

Jessie rubbed seductively against the long length of him, the slick juices from her body moistening his erection. He closed his eyes in an effort to resist her, for he wanted to bring her to orgasm before taking her.

He moved down her body, kissing the soft flesh of her stomach and savoring the scent of musk that emanated from her sex.

She writhed in an attempt to bring him back to her as her mind cried out her displeasure.

For the first time he ignored her, but her insistence that she would disappoint him rose in his mind. This eavesdropping was a challenging sport.

He took hold of her hips as he buried his face in her silken curls. As he stroked her with his tongue, probed the inner recesses of her cleft, he heard her objections fade. Soon her thoughts were a disjointed jumble, spiked with quaking excitement that built with each caress. He knew exactly which of his tricks she liked best from her wild breathing and the encouragement she silently sent him.

But as she neared her climax, he recognized that he would feel it, as well. Her excitement was his excitement, and for the first time since he was a boy, he knew the cold sweat of fearing he would spill his seed before entering her.

She gasped as she climbed up the final peak and then cried out. The clenching, rippling excitement that rolled through him was like nothing he had ever experienced. He went still and found himself arching with her pleasure.

Jessie grasped his shoulders and pulled, dragging him up to her. She spread her legs wide and guided him into her slick cleft. He slid deep into the warm flesh that still rippled with her orgasm.

It was too much. He pumped hard as she gripped his hips with her strong legs. Her fingers raked his back as she murmured encouragement he did not need.

As he felt himself reach his climax, he reared up on his arms so he could see her face. She stared at him in shock and he knew she felt it, too. She felt the rush of heat and pleasure and this triggered another rippling contraction within her. They came together, staring in wonder into each other's eyes.

As the pleasure ebbed, his muscles grew weary and he collapsed beside her, still joined at the hips.

"What in the name of heaven and earth was that?" she asked.

Nagi did not understand it. He had taken possession of thirty men and used them to copulate with their women. Five of them were already with child, since he easily upset their primitive methods of contraception.

But not one of these women had borne *his* child.

Both Niyan and Tob Tob had fathered a Halfling race. True, they did not require possession, having more corporal bodies. Was that the problem?

He went to Tob Tob, on the guise of asking his advice about the running of his circle.

Nagi found the great bear loping through the Spirit World, catching salmon at a sacred river.

The bear could not speak, but Nagi understood his thoughts.

They greeted each other and Nagi posed his mundane questions. The bear sat heavily on the bank, quite taken back. In all the centuries, Nagi had never sought him out, but he did his best to answer, reminding Nagi that his expertise was the care of those who walked on four legs, not two.

"Well, my ghosts don't really have legs anymore." The conversation lagged. Nagi made his excuses, and then, as if in an afterthought, he turned back to Tob Tob.

"I ran into one of your Halflings on earth, an Inanoka named Sebastian. He's a fine boy."

Tob Tob looked confused. The bear was not the brightest in the Spirit World. Finally he brightened.

Yes, I recall a time when I walked the earth and was attracted to human females. Long ago now. My children still walk the earth?

"They do, as do their descendants. They follow

the path of their sire and protect animals from the intervention of men."

Tob Tob bellowed his approval. *I taught them this. I am pleased. They still follow my teachings.*

"How did you do it, exactly? Sire them."

Took human form, of course, and courted them. They have to love you, as I recall—the humans, I mean. A race, you say? I shall have to look into that.

Nagi saw his blunder. He had gained the knowledge he sought, but now the oaf was curious.

"Well, they've gone on for centuries without you. And you like it best here. No hurry." Nagi pointed a wispy appendage toward the stream. "There's a big one!"

Tob Tob turned back to his fishing and did not note the shadow's disappearance.

Nagi slipped down the Way of Souls and back to his dark circle.

Love, he had said. The female would have to love him to conceive. Or would she only have to love who she believed him to be? Nagi shimmered in anticipation, for he loved a loophole.

Chapter 17

Nick gripped Jessie, dragging her to him. What had he just done?

In his madness, he had revealed to Jessie and any of Nagi's sentinels just what this woman meant to him. The truth was, she meant more to him than even he had realized.

"Jessie," he whispered.

She startled awake and he read her thoughts. First, there was her fear of danger and then the realization that she lay safe in his arms. Her contentment at herself in this position tightened his abdomen and he felt the stirrings of desire again.

Great Spirit—his soul mate.

He had known she was special, even recognized that he had stupidly fallen in love with her. But now he understood that she was not a woman he could ever leave behind. She was *his* woman, *his* destiny.

He felt unworthy. All the other women had seen only his human form. Only his mother knew the truth and the knowledge made her hate him. How could Jessie love him when even his own mother had not?

The truth of it burned him to ashes. He was unworthy of this woman, any woman.

He released her, breaking the connection between them, and rolled to his feet, calling the energy to transfigure into clothing and boots.

Jessie frowned, sitting to retrieve her shirt and drag it over her head. Then she scrambled into her jeans.

Nick leaned down and retrieved the pink circle of lace, extending it to her on one finger.

She accepted it gingerly, careful not to touch him, and stuffed the panties roughly into her pocket.

"Why did she loathe you so?"

He frowned. "What?"

"Your mother. She despised you."

Nick absorbed the blow that took away his words.

"How do you know that?"

"You were just thinking it. I heard you." She stood before him, her breathing coming in fast, frantic pants. "Nick, what's happening to us?"

"More than just a new challenge, he said," murmured Nick.

"Who?"

"Tuff. He knew, the bastard. Why didn't he warn me not to touch you?"

All his life women had tried to cage him and he had

avoided their snares with the grace of his kind. Now he'd stepped in a trap far more dangerous and he'd never suspected a thing. How could he have guessed that with one simple touch everything would change? There was no hiding his feelings now. She knew them, felt them as surely as she felt her own.

Instinct took over.

He was already on the opposite stream bank when she called to him. He paused and watched her as she ran down the bank, her bare feet flashing against the green grass. She was lithe and graceful. She would have made a fine deer.

She splashed through the shallow water, threw her arms about his neck and wept. His emotional chaos ignited with her turmoil and they broke apart.

She wrung her hands before her as tears streaked her cheeks. "I knew you couldn't be so cruel. I knew you weren't like your father. Why wouldn't you tell me?"

The tragedy of their love broke his heart. She drew away, carefully severing the contact between them.

"If they're watching, they know," she whispered.

He nodded. "I can't leave you now. It's not safe."

He wanted to hold her but feared this bond forged at contact and so held himself back.

"I'll protect you, Jessie. They won't hurt you. I swear." Her eyes streamed tears, and he flicked them away with a thumb, feeling the sizzle of contact. "You know what this means?"

She nodded. "Soul mates."

"Yes."

"This changes everything," she whispered.

He couldn't deny the truth. They had found each other and there would be no breaking their connection. Together or apart, it existed. Their bond would be hard on her, very hard. He felt guilty for what her love would cost her.

His friend's wife had managed only because she did not know what she was until after she loved him. So alien were the ways of her people that she found it easy to reject them outright.

But Jessie was a member of her community, and until she met him, she was the perfect Spirit Child citizen.

Her association with him would shatter all that. That was assuming he could keep her alive long enough for them to find out.

Chapter 18

Jessie glanced at him repeatedly as they climbed the bank and headed back toward the barn. As they walked, her mind raced ahead. She understood everything now. At their first touch, her confusion had melted and fused into understanding at what Nick was trying to do, his cruel rejection just a ruse to protect her life and keep her from shame. It only made her love him more.

He was the last man on earth she would have chosen, yet fate had intervened. She would not reject the gift the Great Mystery had given her. She was not afraid to face his enemies as long as he was with her.

Apple Blossom, her black-and-white paint stood at the rail of the pasture fence, craning her neck and whinnying. Jessie smiled.

"I have to see to the horses."

"I'll help."

They reached the barn and Nick loaded the bale of hay onto the utility vehicle as she measured the oats. They rode side by side to the hayrack. But despite her shaking the grain bucket, the mares stayed at the far side of the pasture.

"What's gotten into them?" she asked.

"Maybe they smell wolf."

Her jaw dropped in understanding. Of course they would. They knew what Nick was even if she had forgotten.

"Maybe if you leave the pasture."

He swung out of his seat but hesitated.

"You're shivering," he said.

She hadn't realized she was cold until he mentioned it. But her jeans were soaked from the knee down from her romp across the stream and her boots squished when she walked.

He dragged off his shirt and gave it a shake. "Take this."

The shirt had been transformed into a hooded leather sweatshirt, just her size.

She accepted the offering, shrugging into the soft folds that still held his scent and his heat. Jessie smiled up at him. "Be right back."

He zipped up the jacket and lifted the hood, covering her head, then gave the cords a sharp tug. "Call if you need me."

She took the opportunity to watch him walk away. Her heart ached in her chest. He was such a beautiful man.

"Great Mystery, I'm the luckiest woman alive," she

whispered, shaking the grain bucket with more force than necessary.

Her mares watched her break apart the hay bail. Apple Blossom came first, as usual, leading the others. But she stopped well away from the hayrack.

Jessie glanced back at Nick and he lifted his hands up in a gesture of resignation.

Jessie poured the grain into their three buckets, knowing Apple Blossom would finish first and then bully the others, usurping any leftovers. She often put the boss mare in her paddock for dinner, but not tonight. The other two would just have to eat quickly or settle for hay.

Nick had a foot up on the bottom rail and his arms were folded on the top one. He cast her a smile that thrilled her.

She glanced toward her mares. The light was fading, but she could see the three standing still against the far side of the fence. Only their tails moved, beating back and forth in a steady rhythm to discourage the flies.

"Dinner," she called, rattling the buckets again.

The herd remained where it was.

"For goodness' sakes," she muttered. *Must be Nick,* she decided. They could likely smell him from there. She set out with the grain, walked toward them beside the low roof of the extension that had once housed chickens.

Something hit her from behind with enough force to drive her to the ground. There was a deep throaty growl and something seized her head.

Across the pasture the horses began to scream.

The creature shook her, trying to break Jessie's neck. She could feel its fangs and smell the fetid breath. The stink of rot and decay made her gag. And all the while her horses were screaming.

She felt a shuddering vibration the same instant she heard the thud of impact. The creature released her. Jessie dragged her legs beneath her, every muscle of her back and neck throbbing from the assault.

Run, shouted the voice inside her head. She succeeded in standing and then turned toward the sound of struggle to see what had thrown her so violently to the ground.

Nick strained to subdue a huge tawny cat.

A mountain lion!

No wonder the horses were screaming. Nick rained blows upon the lion's sides, each punch accompanied by a sickening crunch.

Why didn't he transform? As a wolf he'd have more speed and his fangs. The cat would feel more threatened by its natural enemy.

The lion succeeded in taking a wicked swipe at Nick. But he dodged it, just outside the length of the cat's reach, the menacing claws narrowly missing his face.

Jessie gasped and then ran, but not toward safety. No, her instincts took her toward the lion, toward Nick, who had succeeded in wrapping his legs about the creature, pinning it to the ground as the feline writhed like a snake.

"Jessie!" he called. "Get back. Run."

It was then that she saw the ghastly yellow eyes. They turned on her, fixing with unnatural calm. Then the cat clawed the earth in an effort to reach her. Nick held fast.

Possessed. Only a sick or starving animal would come so close to man.

Her horses raced along the fence, trying to escape the threat, and she stood frozen, too frightened of the ghost cat to move forward and to afraid for Nick to run away.

Nick tried to choke the cat. The lion was twisting and heaving in a mad effort to get claws or teeth into Nick.

Jessie glanced frantically about for a weapon and spotted her UTV and remembered the bailing hook. She ran, reaching the passenger seat. Gripping the wicked-looking hook of metal that terminated in a perpendicular wooden handle, she charged back across the pasture, holding the hook aloft.

Nick saw her coming. "Throw it."

She did. It landed on the ground beside his head. The cat was now on top of him, struggling to disembowel him with its hind legs. Nick grappled for the weapon, lifted it high and swung it in an arc.

Jessie looked away. The lion screamed. She couldn't keep herself from glancing back. Nick now kneeled over the cat, driving the hook deep into its tawny side. It shuddered as the blade pierced its heart.

Jessie pressed her hand across her mouth to keep from screaming. She'd never seen anything so horrible.

There was a sizzling sound, like bacon on a hot skillet, and then an eerie green glow radiated from the lion. The next instant it went limp.

Nick stood and retrieved the hook. It was then she noted he was still shirtless and his torso was streaked with blood.

Whose blood?

"Nick!" She rushed forward, throwing her arms about him. "Are you hurt? Did it… Are you all right?"

He dropped the weapon and dragged her to his side, glancing back at the horses.

"Come away, now. Quickly."

"But it's dead."

He didn't stop as he rushed her across the pasture and through the gate.

Only then did he turn and face her. He dragged the hood from her head and raked his fingers through her hair.

She felt his anxiety at the attack and the possibility that she might be injured.

"Just frightened," she said.

"Are you sure?"

"Yes." She extended her arms out to show him. "This jacket protected me. It's a miracle that the cat's fangs didn't puncture it." A realization struck her. "This coat, it's a part of you. Isn't it?"

He nodded.

She stared at him. "You couldn't transform, because you gave me half your skin."

"I told you I'd protect you."

"At your expense! Don't do that again, Nick." She slid off the jacket and extended it to him. "I mean it."

His eyes narrowed. "Why?"

"For the same reason you gave it to me. I want to protect you, too."

He wrinkled his brow in disbelief. "Really?"

"Yes, really." She glanced back. "I have to see if my horses are safe. I'll bring them in tonight."

"No."

"But—"

"No, I said. The ghosts could use one or all of them next and I will have to kill them, just like the lion."

His hand clasped hers and she understood everything. The ghosts could possess her precious horses, use them to attack her. She gave a cry of horror as he dragged her along.

"Ghosts do not leave their host unless it is dying or if forced out by a powerful healer. Do you understand?"

"You had to kill it." Jessie began to tremble.

"Yes. They know of our bond. They know it is my duty to protect you."

He gripped her hand and pulled her along. His thoughts crashed into her as they reached the road.

He felt responsible for his father's death. He did not want to be the cause of hers, as well. They ran across the lawn and to the front steps.

"If they had injured you, I would bring you to the Healer, even at risk of his life. They would use you to force me."

"We can't let that happen."

He set them in motion again, hurrying her through the front door. He rested his hand on her bare neck, guiding her farther into the house.

He slipped his hand away, breaking the connection that allowed her to feel his upheaval, and locked her door.

It wouldn't keep the ghosts out but would keep out most possessed creatures.

The shock and violence of the attack began to sink in and Jessie began to shake, as if she were freezing to death.

He gathered her in his arms. She felt his resolve to keep her safe.

His open shirt revealed the blood that now dried on his skin. Jessie led him to the bathroom and wrung out a facecloth. Gently, she washed away the evidence of the attack, finding no mar or puncture in his smooth, taut skin. His stomach twitched as she washed below his navel. Her little finger brushed his flesh.

She could sense his thoughts changing from lions to a memory from his dream of tangled bedsheets and the musky scent of their lovemaking.

Jessie pressed her hand flat to his stomach, savoring his memories and relaying her desire to have him once more.

Chapter 19

Jessie stripped out of her wet clothes and slipped into a silk robe, then led Nick to her bedroom, their palms pressed tight. She released him to flick on the bedside lamp, allowing her to see him, and realized that he did not need the light to see her.

He sat before her on the corner of her bed, his long legs stretched out before him and open for her to step between them.

"Life would be simpler for you if you had let me go," he said.

"I couldn't."

"Why?"

She smiled. "I think I already knew."

He rewarded her with his smile. It did things to her insides. The room suddenly felt a few degrees warmer. She wanted to go to him, but there was more to say.

"Nick, when I first saw you, I thought you were a monster. I don't believe that anymore."

His smile vanished so quickly, she wondered if it had been there at all. "You were right the first time."

"Don't say that." She stepped closer but he lifted his hand to stop her.

"But it's true, or at least, I have the capacity for it. It's in my blood, as you said."

"You aren't like him."

"You just witnessed what I'm capable of."

She was unable to keep from quivering at the memory of the strength and brutality of his attack.

"We are shunned by your people and feared by man for good reason. My kind is solitary. I have been alone over decades. Yet you are so eager to offer me your heart."

She dropped her gaze as his words hit. She was eager. He was the most appealing man she had ever met. Physically, he was unmatched. But it was the mind connection that drew her; the honesty of that joining was unlike anything she had ever known.

She reached for his hand and confirmed her suspicion as his thoughts flowed to her. "But you think my love won't last. That I'll hurt you or use you, like she did."

Nick slipped his hand free as she sat beside him. "Jessie, lots of women find me attractive because they can't see what I really am. If they could, they would run away screaming."

Jessie stilled, knowing this was not entirely true. Humans would be terrified and her people, likely repulsed, but what about his own kind? What about a lithe, beautiful raven.

"What about other Inanoka?"

He hesitated a moment too long and she felt the tearing in her heart.

"My kind do not forgive failure and I am the son of the most notorious Skinwalker who ever lived. It makes me an outcast among them."

"What about Tuff?"

"A holy man, above such emotions."

"You have no true friends?"

Another long pause. "Few. And now I have you and this connection between us that I do not understand. But it gave me hope that you would be different."

She stalked to the dresser and then back as their roles reversed as she hunted him. "I *am* different. Because I am the *first* woman to ever see what is in your heart and it makes me want you more."

He drew back. "It's a mistake."

She had no way to win this argument. She wondered if knowing what was in her thoughts would convince him. Jessie stood and untied her robe, allowing it to fall open, revealing herself to him. His gaze turned hungry as she came to him, taking his head between her hands and pressing his cheek to the naked swell of her breasts. She held him there, with his skin pressed to her own. Could he feel her heartbeat?

Could he feel her change of heart? Did he know that she was not like his mother and that she would never, ever stop loving him?

He drew back, gripping her hands as he gazed up at her.

"With you it is more than the wanting."

She smiled. "Much more."

He closed his eyes and inhaled, his face taking on a pained expression. "I can't resist you."

"Maka be blessed."

His hands slipped from hers and he seized her hips, dragging her forward so that his teeth could scrape the sensitive skin of her breast.

He reached to her shoulders and pushed the silky fabric away, allowing it to fall at her feet.

Nick stood before her, and when she lifted her arms to embrace him, she discovered he was already naked.

"That's hard to get used to," she whispered and stepped into his arms. "But I like it."

He dragged her up against him and then carried them back onto the middle of her king-size bed.

"This is a lot of territory for someone that so often sleeps alone."

She always slept alone and with good reason. Pride made a denial spring to her lips, but then he laughed again and she saw the futility of lies. He saw the truth in her.

"I'm not alone anymore," she whispered.

For the first time in her life, she did not have to hide what she was or what she wanted. He knew everything.

"Better still, I know how to give it to you." His smile made promises he intended to keep.

They grinned at each other.

"That sounds…intriguing." She leaned forward and licked the shell of his ear and plucked his earlobe into her mouth. She sucked it and his thrill of excitement pulsed through her. The reaction so startled her, she drew back to stare down at him in wonder. "This is amazing."

He frowned. "It was…"

She sat up so that she knelt over him, with one knee pressed to each side of his lean hips. "So impatient."

He thrust his hips, bucking hard enough to lift her completely off the bed. When she came back down, his erection was nestled between his belly and her thighs. She gasped in surprise and he laughed.

He was so powerful. He could do whatever he wanted to her and she would let him. But right now she wanted to command him, hold him, make him do her bidding. Even if it were all an illusion. She wanted him under *her* control.

He grinned and lifted his arms. But instead of taking her as he wanted, he pressed his wrists together as if they were bound and placed them above his head.

"Go ahead," he coaxed. "Control me."

She slipped her hands over his wrists and pinned them down. He made a show of testing his bonds, flexing his muscles so she could see the power she sought to contain. His grin was wicked and it did things to her insides.

Jessie's hand glided along his erection, and for the first time, he lost control. He sucked in a breath through his teeth and arched back to increase the contact between them. She felt his urge to grasp her hips and thrust deep inside her.

"So impatient," she murmured, using his words against him.

He growled but relaxed his arms, pressing them back to the mattress. She continued her game, gliding her slick cleft along the full length of him and watching the blood vessels in his neck and forehead pulse. He was losing the battle of restraint, and she knew she could not push him much further.

She leaned forward to kiss him but decided to bite his lower lip instead and then held the soft, ripe tissue between her lips.

He bucked against her, increasing the delicious friction and making her suck in a breath. The gasp inadvertently freed him from her bite. He lifted his head and took her mouth in a deep kiss. One hand slipped from hers, and he clasped her head, bringing her closer and controlling the kiss. She pulled back, sliding away to sit on his thighs.

His erection sprang up between them like a catapult and he looked confused for an instant, then narrowed his eyes and returned his wrist to her possession.

"You'll be sorry," he said. The threat only excited her as she thought of what he might do in retaliation.

"I hope so," she whispered and leaned forward to capture his lips again.

He moved so quickly that she did not have time to react. One moment she was brushing the tips of her breasts across the bare skin of his chest and the next he had captured her breast in his mouth. She arched back at the flood of pleasure cascading through her. Jessie clutched at his head, pressing him tight, forgetting to imprison his wrists.

He moved from one aching breast to the next, loving her and laving her hot flesh with his tongue. She pulsed with desire and wetness, wanting to feel him driving deep.

"Now, please now," she urged.

He pinned her with hungry eyes. "If you want me, then take me."

She had never wanted anything more. Jessie rose up before him, gripping his shaft with both hands as she took possession of him. In the low light, his eyes took on a strange green cast, like the glint of an animal's in the headlights. She held him at the ready as she rose above him. He watched her progress and she felt the restraint he exercised as she began her descent. He wanted to move, to possess, to join, yet he held himself motionless as she glided all the way down until her bottom pressed to his lean hips.

She smiled down in triumph. "You're mine now."

"Always," he whispered.

She began a slow, tortuous rocking as Nick folded his hands behind his head and let her use his body to slake her desire. The friction was delicious but she ached to feel his hands upon her. His eyes met hers and the knowing shone in his confident expression.

He unlocked his hands and reached for her, his fingers working magic as she rocked back and forth. She panted and gasped as her body responded to his touch. She trembled, afraid her legs would not hold her, carry her to the finish she desired. Still his fingers danced over her swollen flesh as he rose to suckle at her swaying breasts. The touch of his mouth was the catalyst that ignited her rising passion. She cried his name and arched, locking her hips tight to his as her release pulsed all around him.

He waited, still, erect, moving just enough to extend her pleasure to the last wave of fulfillment.

She opened her eyes to stare in wonder at her lover. "That was—"

She never had a chance to finish her thought for he flipped her over with such speed that she was dizzy. Throughout, he remained locked deep inside her, but now he arched, pressing her down to the comforter with the lean, muscular power of his loins.

"And now, Dream Child, *you* are mine."

"Yes," she breathed.

He captured her hands and forced them over her head. She was weak from her release and offered no resistance as he clasped her wrists in one hand, using the other to arouse her, stroking her belly and breasts, making her writhe with renewed passion. And all the while he pinned her with his hips and with his hand.

The muscles of his cheeks bulged. She marveled at the tension that he held as he awakened her need until she was bucking beneath him and pleading for him to take her again.

Only then did his control snap. She felt it break and with it came the rush of madness that overcame all rational thought.

She bucked; he plunged. She ungulated; he possessed.

He was a rising firestorm of passion. And instead of holding back, protecting herself, she spread her legs wider, allowing him to touch her as no one ever had.

He seemed to recognize it, for there was a flicker of understanding and his eyes snapped to meet hers. It was then she felt his release begin. She registered it with a gasp as she experienced his passion and, in doing, was rocked by her own.

The combination of emotions shook her and she lost all sense of where they were. She knew only that she was his and he was hers. They had found each other and she would never, ever be the same again.

Her body went slack and he drew her close, cradling her in his arms as he stroked her from neck to hip. His hand made a slow, meandering journey that soothed her jangled nerves. And Jessie allowed herself the pleasure of sleeping in his arms.

Jessie gently basked in the starlight of an unfamiliar meadow and wondered whose dream she visited. She had not intentionally jumped. Something was different here. She was not the observer, but it clearly was not her dream.

Then came a scent. Something new, yet familiar. Elk. Yes, that was it. She breathed deep and then lowered herself to all fours, crouching to listen for her quarry.

Mist clung to the ground, making the elk seem to float above the earth. The fresh, clean fragrance of grass and earth enveloped her.

She lifted her head to find her prey. The dawn was

still hours away, yet she could see everything with such clarity.

The doe beside its mother was young and tender.

Her mouth watered. It had been a long time since the last kill. Behind her, the pack circled silently in the tall grass, shielded by the mist, careful to stay downwind of their prey. They would wait for her to make the first move. She was the alpha and they did as she commanded.

She rushed forward in an explosion of force, streaking with a speed that thrilled her, her muscles powerful and fast as her paws ate up the ground between them.

The elk had seen her now, even half covered as she was by the mist. The mother bolted away, charging into the circle of the others, realizing too late she was trapped. The elk lowered her antlers, preparing to defend her young.

Her pack closed in, growling as the elk pawed the ground. One of the others snapped at the newborn. The mother turned to defend her calf, leaving her haunches exposed to Jessie.

She leaped, biting deep and feeling the hamstrings shred beneath her fangs. Screaming filled the clearing as the others closed in to rip and tear as the elk fell. The young one escaped.

Jessie turned to give chase. Instead she looked at her hands, a trick she often used to control her dream. She saw them coated with the blood of the mother.

"No," she whispered.

Her scream tore her from the dream. She was in her bedroom again. Beside her, Nick leaped from the bed, crouching in a posture, ready to attack. She screamed again, recoiling to escape him. He did not leap at her, but stayed between her and the door, searching vainly for some sign of threat and then turning back to her in bewilderment.

Jessie curled against the headboard, her heart pounding in her chest.

Nick placed one knee on the bed. "Jessie, what's wrong?"

He reached for her and she extended her hand, holding him off.

"No! Not yet. Give me a moment to understand what is happening."

He hovered there before her, a dark shadow, as she tried to rein the terror back in. Had it been her dream or his?

This was why she slept alone. Touching another person while she slept often caused her to slip into their dreams. The journeying disrupted her sleep and she woke exhausted.

But that had not happened here. She was not visiting. She had experienced this.

"Nick, were you dreaming?" she whispered, finding herself still breathless from panic.

"Yes." His voice was cautious.

He sat beside her, careful not to touch her. She released her death grip on the bedpost and crept closer.

"What did you dream?" she asked.

"I was hunting."

"Elk?"

His eyes glowed green and feral in the near darkness. "You were there?"

"No. Yes. Oh, I don't understand this."

He stroked her cheek. "Tell me."

"I wasn't visiting your dream. I was you, chasing the elk, tearing its tendons." She clamped her hand across her mouth to stifle her cry of horror.

He said nothing. Jessie needed to see him. She flipped on the light and found him sitting with his head hanging low and his forehead cradled in his hands.

"I've always been able to keep others from seeing this beast I become. But not you." He stared up at her with a look of such utter misery. "I'm sorry I can't shield you from what I am."

Chapter 20

"I am a hunter, Jessie. It is a part of me."

She opened her arms to him and he accepted her embrace.

He drew her in, molding his body to hers.

She nestled against his warm, solid form and felt the tension slowly dissolve.

"Should I sleep in the other room?" he asked.

She shook her head. "I just have to figure out what to do. This never happened before."

Jessie crawled beneath the covers and waited. Nick lay on top of the blankets beside her but she noticed he was careful not to touch her.

He brushed her hair from her face with the gentlest of touches. Then he flicked off the light and moved to the far side of the mattress.

She lay awake for some time, trying to think of how

Ghost Stalker

to keep from slipping into his dreams. She didn't want to wake him like that again. He had been sound asleep and dreaming, only to be roused to what he assumed was another attack on her, to find her cringing from him.

Did he really hunt like that? She stifled the urge to shiver. There was so much about him she did not know.

Jessie dozed at last and awoke at her usual time, just after sunrise. She opened her eyes to find him already awake.

"How long have you been up?"

"About three seconds."

Yet he looked completely alert. She smiled, feeling rumpled and tired. "How do you—"

"Light sleeper." He grinned. "Any more dreams?"

Her night raid boiled to the surface and she dropped her gaze. "I'm sorry about that."

He stroked her bare shoulder. "Don't be. We are still strangers in many ways."

"No, don't say that."

His sad smile echoed the doubt that haunted her. Was he reluctant to believe her, even when he felt the truth?

She captured his face between her hands, surprised that he did not have the stubble of beard she was accustomed to feeling on a man's face in the morning.

"I love you."

He grimaced and she felt his rising horror. His thoughts jarred her. Love did not last. Love was dangerous. Her love for him would die or be killed by the hatred of her people. They were doomed to repeat his parents' tragic love story.

"I'm not like her."

His eyes were sad but he didn't deny his thoughts. "No, you're not. She was human and had no preconceived notion of how vicious a Skinwalker can be. You, on the other hand, already know."

"Lots of people hunt," she said.

"Not with their bare hands and teeth."

"It doesn't matter."

He swung his feet to the floor and stepped from the bed, fully dressed in faded jeans and a tight white T-shirt.

"Jessie, my father tried to destroy your people. He was a killer and I'm his son. How we gonna get past that?"

Jessie spotted her robe on the floor and retrieved it, slipping into the cold, silky shell. "You're not him."

He faced her from across the king-size mattress. "But I'm like him, more than you realize. He saw the buffalo driven to near extinction by man's reckless killing. Your charges have lost the balance that existed for generations. His duty was to protect the animals by fighting their enemies. My duty is the same."

"But he attacked Spirit Children."

"He attacked men. Your people stepped between him and his prey and the war began."

"He was wrong."

"Was he? He sought to reestablish the balance by controlling a race that was devouring the earth like termites in fresh wood."

They stood only five feet apart, but suddenly a chasm between them yawned to eternity.

She could not suppress the horror his words stirred. "You think what he did was right?"

"Not right, but perhaps necessary."

"How can you say that?"

"How can you protect a species that is destroying the planet?"

"They're not a species. They're men."

"Already we stand on opposite sides."

"No, protecting animals and protecting mankind do not need to be mutually exclusive."

He stared back at her, his eyes sad and weary.

"What about your friend—the Healer? He married one of my race. They love each other and have fought together."

"Whether Sebastian and Michaela's love will last is an open question. I wish them well but am a skeptic at heart."

"Sebastian?" A cold uncertainty gripped her innards as the unusual name echoed from her past. "The Healer's name is Sebastian?"

Nick inched around the bed, his face wary but concerned. "Yes. What's wrong, Jessie? You've gone pale."

She slumped to the mattress as Nick rounded the bed, crouching before her.

What had the raven said?

"She said she was going to find Sebastian. That he would want to know."

"Know what? Who did?" Nick reached for her,

grasping her clasped hands. His eyes widened in understanding. "Bess! She was here. When? How long ago?"

"She came before the buffalo. In the night. Last night, just before dawn."

"Twenty-four hours ahead and flying. She's faster than I am, but she won't fly at night. I still have time." Nick released her and pressed his hands to his forehead.

"The ghosts might have heard her, too. They're following her," said Jessie.

Nick met her gaze and the somber expression told her he already understood this.

"She's leading them to Sebastian and to Michaela." His hands fell to his sides. "Oh, Sweet Mystery—the babies."

Jessie sprang off the bed. "Nick, you have to warn her. You have to stop her from reaching them."

He stood, torn. "I can't leave you. It's not safe."

"Can I come with you?"

"It would slow me. I might not reach her in time."

She drew a heavy breath. "Then you must go."

"I won't leave you unprotected."

"Then call Tuff back."

He wrinkled his brow. "He could be miles away by now."

"He said he'd stay close. Call him."

"I will," said Nick.

She breathed a sigh of relief.

"And you must go to your parents."

She had the sudden image of a firing squad. She stiffened, cinching her robe more tightly. "What?"

"They will protect you in my absence."

He didn't understand her mother. Jessie's stomach roiled with a category-five acid storm.

He studied her reaction and his expression went deadly. She caught her breath, suddenly afraid.

"Are you saying they will not protect their own child?"

That was exactly what she meant. But before she admitted it, she recognized two things. The first was that his own mother had used Nick to seek revenge on his father and that he thought this the most despicable act imaginable. And second, that he would not leave her if he believed she was not safe. And so she lied.

"Of course they will protect me. I just would rather stay here."

He narrowed his eyes at this. "Then we will wait for Tuff."

She was happy that he did not touch her and so could not perceive her deception.

"That could take hours."

He pressed his lips together in a show of stubbornness. "Then so be it."

"Nick, please, you have to hurry."

"No." He sat on the bed.

Jessie was certain her mother would know what her daughter had been up to the instant she saw her. She had always been able to tell, and it often made Jessie's life difficult. Still she would play the charade through. She would allow Nick to come with her to her parents' place. They lived thirty minutes south of her home. She hoped that Nick would be gone before the earth started shaking. When Nick arrived, her father had been away and her mother had not seen the isolated storm the Thunderbirds had caused. This time would be different.

Jessie threw off her robe and burrowed into a turtleneck sweater and a pair of slacks.

"I'll be ready in two minutes," she said, heading for the bathroom.

A few minutes later they had thrown a bale of hay to the horses and were driving her battered Ford F-150 toward her parents' fourteen-acre farm, which was inhabited by one cow, two horses, an angry rooster named Giblet and her two Niyanoka parents.

Nick permitted her to drop him just short of the property line. Jessie then pulled in the drive and parked. He waited by the tall grass at the roadside for her to let herself in. She stood inside the door and waved him off, hoping he would be gone before her parents knew of her arrival.

Nick stood by the rusty barbed-wire fence, watching her until she disappeared inside the neat yellow house, and then turned and ran out into the open pasture, jumping the four-foot fence without breaking stride. The horses charged in the opposite direction, making for the barn as he called the winds. He needed to get far enough from the structures not to threaten them. He needed to get to Bess and prayed he was not too late.

The winds gusted, violently shaking the treetops. He gazed toward the overcast sky, seeing the vortex open in the clouds. Black swirling fingers reached down for him, snatching him as cleanly as an eagle captures a salmon.

The icy air filled his lungs, and all about him the air was full of the thunder from the beating of mighty wings.

"Jessie," her father shouted from inside the house. "Is that you?"

She stood in stunned silence, watching Nick fly up into the arms of the Thunderbirds, wondering what it was like to soar with those mighty creatures.

The gravity of her blunder settled over her with the dust. She was so absorbed in watching the twister touch down that she did not hear her mother's approach until her gasp brought Jessie about.

Her mother had seen such clouds during the war and Jessie could tell by the pallor of her mother's face that she knew exactly what was in that storm.

"It's happening again," her mother whispered.

"No, Mom, it isn't. He's a friend."

The stinging slap across her cheek brought her eyes up to meet her mother's angry glare.

"You brought it here! Exposed us to them?"

Tears welled in Jessie's eyes as she pressed her hand to her throbbing cheek. "No. Listen."

"It's our only protection, our invisibility. I've taught you this. How could you?" Her mother's face was flushed, and the vessels bulged and pulsed in ugly serpentine tubes across her forehead.

Jessie hardly recognized her. "You don't understand."

"I do! That was a Skinwalker! And you called him friend." Her mother was shrieking now.

It was what Jessie had feared, this kind of ugly confrontation with her mother, and now that it was actually happening, she felt strangely detached.

Her father reached for his wife, but she tried to shake him off, before collapsing into his arms, sobbing.

"Oh, what has she done?"

"Easy, Mother. It's gone."

"It knows where we live! It might come back and kill us while we sleep."

"No. He wouldn't. Mom, I trust him."

Her mother spun again, looking feral and ready to attack. "Trust? Those murderers?"

Her father stared at Jessie over his wife. "Does anyone else know about this?"

"No."

"Then we can fix it."

Jessie knew she should be ashamed, contrite and apologetic. But something in her father's vow to fix her little indiscretion infuriated Jessie. She wondered what made them right and her wrong. Really, why was it impossible to love a man as noble, fearless and devoted as Nick?

Her mother was sobbing again. Her father glared at Jessie.

"See what you've done?" He patted his wife's back. "We're safe now. It's gone and she won't ever see it again. Isn't that right, daughter?"

"No. That's not right."

Her father's mouth dropped open. She did not know

which of them was more astonished, her father or herself.

"He's more than a friend. His name is Nick and he walks as a wolf."

The three stared at each other for a moment as the realization that everything had changed pulsed between them like a dying heart. And then her mother lunged at her. Jessie jumped back and her mother swept past.

She rounded on Jessie, fists flailing. "I'll kill you myself before seeing you with a wolf."

Jessie ducked and her father grabbed her mother.

"You don't know him," said Jessie, still trying for the impossible.

Her mother's laugh was a fearful sound. "Oh, I do."

"He's protecting the last Seer of Souls."

Her mother hesitated and she and her father exchanged a look.

"Lies!" hissed her mother.

"Mother, the rumors," said her father.

"No, I said."

Jessie's eyes narrowed. "You've heard of her."

Her parents were suddenly silent.

"What rumors?"

It was her father who broke the silence.

"Word came from Seattle that a Niyanoka was seen in the company of a bear several months ago. But she refused help, choosing to stay with a Skinwalker."

"But she claimed to be a Seer," said Jessie, leaning forward toward her father as if his answer could not come fast enough.

Her father nodded. "The council rejected the report as false. It *has* to be false."

"Because she chose to stay with her husband?" asked Jessie.

Her mother's voice was an angry hiss. "Because no Niyanoka would *ever* choose a Skinwalker as a mate."

Her mother's eyes dared Jessie to say otherwise.

"But she did and so our people abandoned her."

"*She* abandoned *us*."

"Did they offer help?"

"Of course they did. She refused."

Jessie snorted. "Protection from her husband when Nagi still hunted her? *Is* still hunting her."

"How do you know that?"

"The Skinwalkers told me."

"You have spoken to more than one?" Her mother's voice remained sharp as a shard of glass. "Have I not told you their trade is lies?"

"I was attacked by a possessed mountain lion. I saw the ghost leave its dead body. This is no lie."

Her father paled. "We must warn the council. If a ghost attacked one of our own, they must know."

"But then they'll know she has been with a wolf." Her mother waved her hands before her in a gesture of dismissal. "There is no Seer. There was no attack." She pointed a finger in Jessie's face. "Do you know what will happen if any of the others learn of this?"

Jessie knew. To fraternize with the enemy was to face banishment from her community. The gravity weighed upon her. Once the others learned of her disgrace, her parents would have to shun her or lose their place in the community. By choosing Nick, she would bring shame on her parents.

She glanced at the sky, wondering if Nick would find Bess in time.

"Are you even listening to me?" asked her mother.

Everything was as it had been before the winds had dropped Nick at her feet. Only she had changed.

The path she had thought to walk all her life had become a charade. She no longer wanted to be one of them—not if it meant giving up Nick. Her duty to her race faded when faced with her duty to the last Seer. The Skinwalkers were not the threat, Nagi was, but only she knew the truth.

She had already chosen her place and she was sorry only for the pain she would cause her mom and dad.

She would follow Nick's example and fight Nagi.

Without realizing the exact moment it had happened, Jessie had already left them.

"Nick wanted me here because he is afraid the ghosts might hurt me again, use me to force him to seek the Healer."

Her mother's eyes widened, but she refused to fold. "There are no ghosts!"

"Let her in, Mother," said her dad.

"Not unless she assures us that she will never see this monster again."

Jessie felt sad and tired and disappointed that her enlightened parents were so sure of what they believed that they would entertain no doubt.

"I can't do that."

"Then I'll have nothing more to do with you." Her mother actually pointed down the steps. "Get out."

Jessie nodded, accepting their decision. "Goodbye, Mom. Bye, Dad."

Jessie drove back to her place, and found three ranchers waiting beside their truck. She recognized them from town. Cal and Carlos and the third name she could not recall, but all were hands on the Diamond Bar.

They were well dressed for a Saturday night and waiting beside their spotlessly clean truck. One held a clipboard, making her wonder if they were after signatures for some political initiative. She slid from the truck, thinking it was filthy by comparison, and then paused, feeling suddenly uneasy.

"Hello, boys." She kept a hold on the open door, standing between it and her cab. The forced smile died on her lips as she noted the glowing yellow eyes.

Ghosts, she realized and slid back into the vehicle, slamming the heavy door shut as they reached her. With a touch of a button she locked the doors. All three faces filled the window. One rattled the door handle as she fumbled in her pocket for her keys. Her hands shook as she scrambled to slide the key into the ignition.

As she felt it engage, she closed her eyes and thought of her mother, knowing that she could hear her daughter's cry for help. The engine growled to life and Jessie opened her eyes to see Cal haul back his fist and punch the driver's-side window.

The pane exploded in tiny cubed pieces, cascading over her in a shower of glass. Jessie flung up her arm and screamed. A moment later she was hauled from her seat and dragged through the shattered window, kicking and clawing, toward the unfamiliar truck.

Cal lifted his bloody fist and punched her in the temple. The explosion of light and pain felled her like a tree. She pitched forward onto the possessed men. Stupefied by the blow, she lay limp as a rag doll. Her head lolled, giving her a view of the toes of her boots as they were dragged over the grass and onto the gravel of her driveway. A door opened and they stuffed her into the backseat of the shining blue pickup.

Truck doors slammed and tires squealed.

Jessie struggled with the door and received another vicious slap across her cheek, stunning her. She floated in and out of consciousness as the truck sped through the night. She did not know how much time had passed when she became aware of her surroundings again. They had tied her legs and wrists together. She lay under a greasy blanket on the narrow backseat of the large pickup. The vibration of the engine and the smoothness of the ride made her believe they were on a highway.

Where were they taking her?

She needed help. She closed her eyes and concentrated, breathing the stale air and resting her muscles. Long practice made the relaxation technique second nature. Soon she floated in a state of peaceful well-being.

A moment later she slipped from her physical self, projecting her astral body out to search for Nick.

But she soon realized that the only way to speak to Nick was to visit his dreams. That left only her mother. Would she even listen?

Jessie didn't know, but she had to try.

Chapter 21

The scented trail grew stronger as Nick loped along on the pine-needle loam. It did not matter that Bess traveled in the sky, for his gifts allowed him to find the trail of any living thing he had ever met, over land, water or air. She was faster than he was, but the winds had brought him close. He increased his speed, breaking into a streaking run, until his muscles burned with fatigue.

The scent trail ended so abruptly that he skidded to a halt beneath a huge Douglas fir. He looked up and found her, in human form, reclining on a massive tree branch, like some female Peter Pan. She maintained all her abilities when in human form, which meant she need not worry about falling. He was jealous at times of her gift of flight.

"Hello, Nicholas. You look well."

He called his power to shift, momentarily overcome

by the surge of power blasting through him. Standing now in human form in his cloak, he found Bess already on the ground beside him.

"Did you discard her already?" she asked, the wicked smile curling her full lips.

He did not register her gibe in his rush to speak.

"How close are you to them?" he asked.

"I should think—"

"Don't answer that!"

She scowled. "Nicholas, what has gotten into you?"

"You're being followed."

Bess made the low gurgling sound of a raven's displeasure as she glanced about and, seeing nothing, deferred back to him. Her expression now registered confusion. "Are you sure?"

"A ghost of Nagi's guard."

She gasped. "I can't see them on this side," Bess said, referring to her gift of speaking to souls who had crossed to the Spirit World. Her gift was strong, for only the raven could cross to the other side and return to tell the tale. But not even Bess could see the ones who chose to walk the earth or who were cast from the Spirit Road and into Nagi's realm of the Circle of Ghosts.

"They possessed three humans and attacked me. I heard one shouting not to lose sight of me until I led them to the Healer. The Thunderbirds came and they left their hosts to follow. I can no longer see them, but I know they are near. One attacked Jessie last night."

Bess glanced about and shivered. If anyone knew the power of ghosts, it was Bess. "Why didn't your Niyanoka tell me?"

"She didn't know that Sebastian was the Healer."

Bess made a sound of annoyance.

"I know you, Bess. You said something to insult her, didn't you?"

"The little fool is in love with you. No surprise there. Every female who meets you falls in love with you, Nick. It's as common as bees around a hive. Not that I'm jealous. We all need variety."

"And you told her about us. Didn't you?"

She glanced away. "I didn't say we were a *current* item."

He growled. "Remind me to do the same for you someday."

Bess rarely looked chastened, but she did drop her gaze for an instant. When her dark eyes returned to meet his, she held her chin in defiance.

"What shall we do, then? About Sebastian and Michaela, I mean."

"Stay clear of them."

"Don't you think they should know you were followed and attacked?"

"Not if the telling puts them in danger."

Bess made a noise in her throat. "I never meant to do that. Is it listening right now, do you think?"

"Yes."

She glanced about her. "I hate ghosts."

The two stood under the canopy of the forest in silence for several moments.

"What if I could get a message to Michaela by way of a road that no ghost of Nagi would dare follow?"

Nick knew instantly what she proposed and a wide grin spread across his face. "Would it work?"

"Michaela's father and mother come to her often in dreams. Let them follow and face the judgment." Bess's smile was ruthless.

"But you don't fly at night."

"Oh, no. That is the best time to take this path. It is clearer in starlight."

"Let me know what happens."

"Where will you go now?" asked Bess.

"Back to her." He turned, but Bess placed a hand on his upper arm and he paused.

"Be careful, Nick. The hatred runs in them with their blood," she said.

He pressed his lips together. "I know. But she is different."

Her eyes reflected a pity that made Nick's stomach roll with acid.

"I hope, for your sake, you are right."

He placed his hand over hers and nodded. "Walk in beauty," he said, giving her the traditional parting words of their people.

"And you." She hesitated. "And be watchful. Nagi is a vengeful foe. He has no beating heart and is careless with the lives of the living."

"I will remember your words."

She broke away. Nick watched Bess transform into the glossy raven that called a farewell as she shot through the trees like a living shadow.

He needed to get back to Jessie but could not call the Thunderbirds. It would have been disrespectful. They weren't a travel service. By calling them only in true emergencies, his people had continued to gain their indulgence. The minute that changed, his kind would be grounded like the arrogant Niyanoka.

Transforming into the gray timber wolf, he loped south by starlight, knowing there were few places where he would not find signs of man if he just kept to a straight course. By sunrise he had located a timber road and then an unmarked gravel road. He continued into the morning, searching for pavement and a way back to Jessie.

He believed her parents would protect her, so why did his instincts urge him to hurry.

Michaela dreamed of her babies, new and pink. She slept lightly, listening for their cry, her breasts filling with milk.

But the call she heard was not the thready wail of her hungry offspring, but the soft resonant voice of her mother.

"Congratulations, daughter."

Her mother's ghost had not visited her since before the birth, when she came to reassure her that the twins within her were strong and ready to be born. Michaela had awakened already in labor.

"Oh, they are so beautiful. Can you see them?" she asked.

In her dreams, her mother seemed alive, except for the silver glow about her. It was how Michaela knew she was speaking to a ghost who had crossed to the Spirit World.

"Only their spirits. They are strong and will need to be strong."

Michaela frowned. She did not like to think of her children having a difficult future. Her mother spoke again.

"I come with a message from Bess."

Michaela's breath caught as she considered what this might mean. "Is she dead?"

Her mother laughed. "No, daughter. She simply came for a visit, as a raven may do. She was on her way to find you but discovered she is being followed."

"Who could follow a raven?"

"Only another raven or a ghost," said her mother.

Michaela gasped as cold air seemed to lift the small hairs all over her body.

Her mother's face gave no reassurance. "Nagi is searching for you and the children. He has not given up and he will use your friends to get to you."

"I'm not ready yet." Michaela's gift had been shielded even from herself until very recently. So now her father, who had died to protect her, came to her in her dreams, and he taught her to use her powers.

"I know, daughter, but you must learn your art quickly now so you can keep your darlings safe from the ruler of ghosts."

"Is Nick all right?"

"No, daughter. All of Sebastian's friends are in grave danger. They fight to protect you."

Nagi changed his tactics with the females. This time he seduced a woman without use of a host. This female, just sixteen, was suggestible but physically strong.

His initial contact with her had been successful. She

was from the Hawk Clan, though he did not know if that would matter. He did not think his children would shift like the Skinwalkers or have connections to the soul like the Spirit Children. He was not certain what powers would come to his children. He knew only that they would be mighty. It was a great experiment and he was anxious to begin.

She came to him in the cave that he had chosen for this purpose. In the darkness, she could not see him and that was best. For his appearance was frightening by design.

But here in the inky blackness she would not tremble at his yellow eyes or vaporous body.

The crept forward, her hand raised to protect her face. He swept forward, guiding her with his voice, ushering her farther into the earth. Water seeped down the limestone walls, making the air dank and acrid. Icy water pooled on the floor. It had been difficult to find a dry place for her comfort.

She thought him a god and so he was, but not the god she prayed to, not the burning bush, but one just as ancient and vengeful.

He had learned that using a host body was equivalent to using a condom. The other males prevented him from impregnating his women. This time he would try a different tack.

"Lie on the floor and prepare to receive me."

She did as he bid her, lifting her skirt and folding her hands to pray.

He surrounded her and she gasped, taking in some of his essence in her mouth. He could not really hold her, for his vaporous body was not as tangible as hers, but he could still enter her. Deep inside her womb, he found the tiny waiting egg and merged his essence with hers. Then he detached that piece of himself and withdrew.

Once away from her, he was discouraged to see she was not breathing. This irritated him, thinking he would have to begin again. It had taken days to convince her of his divinity and to gain her willing participation in this joining, and then he'd had to wait for her time of fertility.

He hovered over her still body, wondering what might revive her. Nothing occurred to him, and he was about to abandon her when she gasped, choked and then vomited on the ground.

Nagi shimmered in victory.

"Lord, I see you." The awe in her voice flattered his ego.

"You now carry my child. Guard it well or feel my wrath."

She scrambled to her feet. "Yes, Lord. Thank you, Lord."

He ushered her from the cave, controlling her direction with his mind.

All he must do now was wait to see if his garden bore fruit.

He glowered as he noted one of his ghosts waiting for him outside the cave. His incubator walked right through him, pausing only to rub the chill from her skin before descending the path that would lead her back to her farmhouse and her parents.

Nagi's mood darkened at the sight of his servant.

"Master, I bring news. The wolf was visited by a raven. This one said she would warn the Healer. So I followed her far to the north. But last night the wolf warned her of my presence and she changed course, following the Way of Souls."

Nagi billowed in fury.

"I will kill him!"

"He went south, Lord. But I followed the raven as far as I could."

His anger turned to rage. Both the wolf and raven had slipped away. It could be months, years before he was lucky enough to stumble on them again.

He needed some way to flush him from cover. There was only one creature whose whereabouts he knew. The wolf had saved her once. Would he do so again?

He had to force the Dream Walker to call the wolf and then injure her badly enough so that no creature but a Healer could save her.

"Capture the Dream Walker alive."

"Yes, Master."

The ghost followed the raven high into the night sky, but when he saw the portal gaping wide, he hesitated. He knew where she was heading now and that he could not follow. He had seen this gateway before, just after his death. It had opened for him and he had stood on the brink of the Ghost Road. But he understood his chances. He would never reach the Spirit World without many prayers from his descendants and they did not follow the old ways. His life's deeds were black. How long would he have to circle in the void before his sins were washed clean?

He trembled. If he followed the raven, the old crone would throw him from the path and he would fall into the Circle of Ghosts.

He retreated, back to the earth. Better to be a shade of himself forever than to spend eternity spinning in the Wheel of Sorrow. Should he tell his master what had occurred or flee? He thought of Nagi's vengeance if he were caught.

The ghost changed direction and swept through the night toward Nagi, who still remained on this earthly plain.

Chapter 22

It was a little past six in the morning when Nick called his executive assistant at her home in New York City to arrange for a car.

"Got it," Alison said, her voice crisp and professional despite the unconventional timing of his call. "Will an airport pickup work for you?"

"Yeah."

"Estimated arrival?"

Nick glanced at the tow truck driver who picked him up on Highway 12. "How far to Billings?"

The man readjusted the chaw in his cheek. "Seventy miles or so."

"Feel like a detour?"

The man's gaze swept over him, assessing his expensive clothing, and then he spit. "All right. I'll bite. What'll you pay?"

Nick held his hand over the receiver. "Name it."

"Three hundred bucks."

Nick smiled. "Done." Then to Alison, he said, "Make it an hour."

Nick hung up the phone. "Hope you're a fast driver."

The human's eyes flashed at the challenge. He drew an old toothpick from behind his ear and clamped it in his teeth. "Let's go."

Nick climbed back into the cab of the red tow truck. He meant to stay awake, but he had been twenty-four hours without any sleep and had been running most of that time.

He was dozing in the cab when she came to him.

"Help me!"

It was all he heard, but he knew it was Jessie. He knew that she was in danger and that she was calling him. The urgency of her plea was so jarring that it jolted him awake.

"Where are we?" Nick asked, raking a hand through his hair.

"Nearly there. See? There's the sign."

Nick glanced up at the road sign and then fell back into the seat. He could do nothing on the highway. Even if he did call the winds, he did not know her whereabouts. To find her, he must track her.

He'd drive to Jessie's place and start from there.

The next twenty minutes were pure torture. But he did not doubt his instincts. She had called him, needed him. He prayed that her parents had not been injured defending her. They were Children of Spirit, not warriors. It was why his people had easily defeated them. They lacked the instinct of predators, like his kind. Why had he left her?

What had happened to her parents? Nick mused as he reached the airport and got into the waiting red Mustang.

The road was blessedly clear of traffic at midmorning. He pushed the Mustang, recognizing that it moved faster than he could.

He reached her home to find all three mares with their necks craning over the fence, as if they were looking for their next meal. He pulled into the drive behind the unfamiliar silver Cadillac.

He jammed the car into Park and breathed in the air. Jessie's scent was everywhere, but not fresh. He left the car and walked up the driveway, past the sedan. He paused to scent two passengers, who were unfamiliar; their scent trail was fresher than Jessie's. They had arrived here last night, hours after she had and they had not left.

He continued to her mud-crusted Ford pickup, pausing at the droplets of blood on the gravel. He knelt and inhaled—not hers. He lowered his head to concentrate and followed her. His heart hammered when he stood and saw the shattered glass of the driver's-side window. He leaned into the battered old Ford. She had not been here since early yesterday evening. He scented three unfamiliar humans and the lingering stench of death. He stiffened.

"God damn," he muttered, knowing the ghosts had her. He turned back the way he had come, following them. There were the twin marks in the gravel, but not to this Cadillac. They dragged her. He headed for his Mustang.

"Wait!"

Nick turned toward the house, seeing a man standing in her doorway. Nick lowered his body, preparing to attack.

"I'm Jessie's father."

Nick paused. "Are you or your wife injured?"

He held his breath as he awaited the answer.

"Injured? No, of course not."

Nick frowned. "I sent her to you. Why did she return here alone?"

The man flushed, then climbed down the steps to the stone path. Nick met him halfway.

"Where is she?" Nick asked.

"We hoped you'd know. You're the Skinwalker, aren't you?"

Nick inclined his head. "Why was she back here?"

"Because she has broken our laws."

Nick felt a sickness spread like cancer through his stomach. How could he have assumed that these two would protect their own blood, when his mother had not? "You abandoned her."

"We had no choice. She violated our laws."

Nick turned to go. He had no more time to waste with this man.

Her father followed. "My wife is a Dream Walker, as well. She's been in contact."

Nick paused.

"Jessie is still unconscious. How did you know about the attack?"

"She called me in my sleep."

"Don't be ridiculous. Dream Walkers don't enter the dreams of a…"

"Beast?"

The man glared. "This is your fault."

He didn't deny it as he met the accusation in her father's eyes. "Where is she?"

"We can't get her location until she awakens."

"I can."

Nick turned back toward the scent band that was her essence coursing in a river in her wake. He faced the strong, wide track, invisible to all but Skinwalkers of the wolf clan. "I can find her without you, but it would be helpful to contact her."

Jessie's father looked uncertain. "That would require my wife's consent."

"They're going to kill her."

The older man pressed his lips together and for a moment Nick thought he would do nothing to save her.

"Wait here."

A moment later the door swung open and Nick faced a smaller, darker and only slightly older version of Jessie. The woman's looking figure was trim, and she would have been attractive if not for the descending eyebrows and mouth drawn in a thin bitter line.

"Go away," she ordered.

He turned to go.

"Wait," said Jessie's father.

"George, don't speak to him."

"He's trying to find her, Marta."

Nick paused in the drive. "I can find her without your help."

"Good, because you aren't getting it," snapped Marta.

"Marta, please," said her husband.

Her bottom lip quivered as she glared daggers at Nick. "If they do anything to my girl, I'll hunt you down like the animal you are."

Nick accepted her threat without comment.

"He can track her, Marta," said George.

His wife stared at Nick. "If you can help, you are welcome."

The three regarded each other warily as the uneasy truce formed between them.

Nick returned to his convertible. He waited as George ushered Marta down the drive.

"We haven't met officially." Nick extended his hand, expecting to be shunned. But he wasn't. The hesitation was obvious but the man did shake his hand.

"George Healy."

"Nick Chien." They broke contact.

"This is my wife, Marta."

She glared at him.

Nick opened the door to his Mustang. "Are you coming?"

"I won't sit in a car with him," said Marta to her husband. "He might kill us both."

George's expression looked pained. "We'll follow you."

Nick waited no longer but slipped behind the wheel and followed the familiar scent that would bring him back to Jessie.

Nagi followed his ghost over the meadow, their passing so silent they did not even disturb the mist that hovered over the wet grass.

His ghosts had taken the little Niyanoka far enough that she would not be recognized, but not far enough to make it difficult for the wolf to find her. This time he had more than a dozen ghosts guarding his prize. More than enough for one wolf.

Nagi was anxious to deliver an injury so grave that neither a human nor a Spirit Child could heal it. A wound that would force the Healer's gift.

His soldiers shimmered in salute as he passed with his guide. He reached the cabin on the ranch where she was held and drifted through the wall of the room in which the Spirit Child was bound. On seeing him, his three sentries vibrated to attention.

"Are you certain she is his soul mate?" asked Nagi.

The ghost closest to the woman contracted, glowing a faint greenish brown. "Yes, lord. I heard the wolf say so."

Nagi looked at the still form upon the bed. "What have you done to her?"

The same ghost was quick to reply. "Peko slapped her across the face. She has been still ever since."

Nagi flapped with rage.

He glanced at the woman and then stared hard. Her life force was split.

Nagi spun in a cyclone of fury, pinning the remaining ghost to the wall. "How long has she been like this?"

"A few hours only, lord," gasped his guide.

"She's a Dream Walker, you idiot. And she's left her body. She's trying to get help."

Had she already contacted the wolf? Nagi faced the woman and concentrated, calling her back to this time and place. He needed both halves of her here when he administered the spirit wound. For this one, he would create a grand illusion. She would not know the wolf was safe. From the prison of her mind she would know only what he wanted her to know. And she would believe it was true.

If the wolf wanted her to live, he would have to bring her to the Healer.

Jessie's scent came to Nick, strong and clear as a blood trail. Her fear increased the strength of the signal she left behind. Her trail led him to I-90 going toward Billings.

Nick nodded and pressed his foot farther down on the gas pedal, checking to see if the Healys could keep up.

It was several moments before he realized that a raven was flying high up above them, but mirroring their direction.

Bess?

He hoped so. He'd been sending distress signals to any Inanoka in the area. There could be more than one raven hereabouts but he hoped it was Bess. Could she have been to the Spirit World and back so quickly?

She had told him the journey was unpredictable, sometimes taking moments in earth time and sometimes weeks.

He sped on but traveled so fast that when Jessie's trail veered sharply to the left, he almost missed the turnoff to the J Bar M.

Nick pulled over to the shoulder and waited for Jessie's parents to do the same.

"We're close."

The two looked expectantly at him.

"If you have some method of contacting Jessie, you best do it," said Nick.

Her mother glared at him.

The fire in her eyes reminded him of Jessie, and his heart gave a pang of regret. He softened his voice.

"Tell her we're coming. Find out how many guards she has seen."

"I don't take orders from you."

Nick turned to George. "Can you contact her?"

He shook his head in regret. "My gift is evocation. I'm a Peacemaker."

Nick was unfamiliar with the term.

Mr. Healy turned to his wife and laid a hand on her shoulder. "Mother, please." Mr. Healy closed his eyes. A moment later they snapped open and Nick leaned closer.

"She's in some kind of sleep, but not sleep. I can see from her eyes, but she can't." She turned to her husband, clinging to him. "I don't understand. What have they done to her?"

"Where is she, mother?" asked George.

"In some kind of ranch house. The shades are drawn. She's alone, I think."

George glanced at Nick.

"Could be ghosts there. I can't see them," said Nick. "Can you?"

George shook his head. Both of Jessie's parents peered down the long road, but could see nothing of the ranch that might be at the other end.

George glanced up at the sign. "I know this place. It's a dude ranch. Really swank. Thousand bucks a night for some of the cabins."

"I'm going through the woods. It's faster," said Nick.

George nodded. "We'll try the road. If I run into trouble, I'll make some suggestions. Don't know if they work on ghosts, though." He turned to Mrs. Healy. "Back in the car, Mother."

She glared at Nick. "I want my daughter back."

"Yes, ma'am. I want that, too."

Mrs. Healy stayed where she was, arms crossed tightly before her. "This is all your fault."

George wrapped an arm about her shoulders. "Later, Mother. Let him go now."

Nick studied the two Niyanoka. How old were they? Two hundred years—three? He gauged his strength and thought George no match for what lay ahead. Perhaps it was a mistake letting them come, for they distracted him from his goal. He did not want Jessie's parents killed in this battle.

"Maybe you best wait here," said Nick.

Jessie's father stopped short.

Nick returned his steady stare. It was unfortunate, because his talents could be useful in a fight. Yes, perhaps he might let him come along, but to do so was to leave her mother unprotected. Best bring her, as well.

Nick recalled her father's mentioning the gift of evocation and shook his head to rid himself of the thoughts that were not his own. Nick's thoughts, no longer blocked, came rushing in like a wave, filling the void.

"All right, you've made your point. Will that work on possessed men?"

"I sure the hell hope so."

Not the hearty affirmative Nick was looking for.

The raven landed on the roof of the Mustang.

Mrs. Healy waved her hands at it. "Shoo, shoo."

Nick opened his mouth, but before he could get a word in, the raven faced the woman and spoke in a high, gravelly voice.

"Why don't you shoo. At least I came prepared to fight."

Mrs. Healy staggered back and only her husband's quick reflexes kept her from falling into the gully beside the road.

Bess faced Nick. "I saw Michaela's father. He tells me she has delivered her twins, both healthy. There are two more Seers in the world."

Nick grinned. "Sebastian is a papa!"

"Indeed," said the raven. "He also tells me Michaela's strength and skills are growing. He says she is more powerful than he ever was."

Mrs. Healy recovered her tongue. "She didn't marry a—a Skinwalker."

Bess rotated her head 180 degrees to face the woman. "Yes."

"But that's impossible. They can't have bore children."

Nick leaned on the hood. "Is that what your book of law tells you?"

"Don't you mock our laws, wolf," said Mrs. Healy.

"Seems like you need a codicil or amendment to me," replied Nick.

Bess flapped. "Who are they and why are they here?"

"These," said Nick, motioning to the couple, "are Jessie's parents."

"Oh." Bess's voice, strange as it was, still radiated disappointment.

"Bess, can you fly over that ranch and give me a report? I'll be right behind you."

"We're coming, too." Jessie's father turned to his wife. "Marta, we need help. They're offering."

Her lips pressed tight but she nodded.

He turned to Nick. "We'll be right behind you."

"How close do you have to be to use your gift?" Nick asked George.

"Just within sight. But I'm not allowed to have them hurt themselves. It's against our way."

"Fine." Now Nick turned to Bess. "Go. I'll follow."

Bess lifted off, rising into the air. In a moment, she circled.

"She's over the ranch. You two stay together. I can't speak to you as a wolf, but I understand you."

That said, he drew upon his energy to shift, stretching out into the sleek form of his wolf self. Behind him, Mrs. Healy cried out in terror, but he had no time to waste. He set off for the line of pine at a run.

Nagi hovered before the Dream Walker, waiting for the moment that her body and soul aligned. In that instant he touched her forehead, administering the blow that would split her soul from this husk of a body forever.

Nagi floated back from his victim, undulating with satisfaction. The wolf might find her body, but even a tracker could not follow this trail.

Her astral body hovered above her physical one, gleaming brilliant silver. Here was a soul destined never to drop into his circle.

Still, he could speak to her now.

"Do you love him?" he asked.

The Dream Walker, trapped in his illusion, said yes.

"Then follow him. Hurry, or he will leave you behind."

Chapter 23

Jessie had managed to contact her mother with a distress call but could not tell her where she was. Nick had told her he could track anyone anywhere in the world. If he remembered her visit to his dream he could find her.

The contact had been so brief, only a moment, really, when she had found him dreaming and called for help. He was startled awake so quickly that she did not know if he understood. She had not found him asleep since then.

Dreams were fragile things and a jarring from slumber could shatter them as surely as fine china thrown to a concrete floor.

Please, Nick, come for me.

He could not see her astral body, but she could see him. A visit now might tell her if he understood. She found him running across a parking lot in the near darkness. Pools of blue fluorescent light illuminated the rows of cars. She glanced down and saw the numbers carefully painted at each spot.

Nick dashed past her, toward a black SUV, drawing up short to check the key he held in his hand.

The streetlight beyond where he now stood buzzed and then winked out. The next light followed and then the third. All now glowed a weak orange, casting no light.

Nick turned toward the streetlights, looking about with quick darting glances. Seeing nothing, he continued toward the passenger side. A wind blew past him and he halted again, turning toward the disturbance. And then she saw it.

A gray mass of swirling debris rushed toward him. A Thunderbird? It rose twelve feet in height and changed shape as it approached. Now it more resembled some great smoky ape. Putrid yellow eyes blinked open and she knew with chilling certainty who this was.

Nagi, Guardian of the Circle of Ghosts, had found Nick.

She tried to warn him, but he could not hear her. The thing extended undulating arms, reaching with talons sharp and glossy black.

Nick braced to face this Spirit, but how did a shifter fight a shadow?

Nagi pointed a menacing talon and Nick's body convulsed. Jessie watched in horror as Nick fell to his knees, his chest and stomach split by some unseen force. He pitched forward, falling to the ground behind the car, the circle of blood flowing out before him.

She must find him, reach him before he bled to death. She was about to withdraw when she felt her body, safe but still bound. She could do nothing to save him.

Nagi slid forward, bringing his vaporous arm down. Nick choked, grasping his throat as his feet kicked madly against the rear bumper.

Nick slumped to the ground once more. Jessie's heart broke in two as she realized Nagi had killed him. She watched Nick's soul rise in a wisp of white. Above him the stars glittered more brightly as the Milky Way became a highway to lead Nick along the Way of Souls.

No! But he could not hear her.

She had only just found her soul mate and already he had been taken from her.

Nagi watched her. Could he see her?

"Do you love him?"

She wanted to attack Nagi but knew he was immortal and beyond her rage. *Yes,* she answered.

"Then follow him. Hurry, or he will leave you behind."

Jessie watched Nick's soul retreat. She had always followed the laws of the Dream Walker and so had never before even considered leaving this earthly plane, though at times she thought she glimpsed this portal to the Spirit World. But she did not hesitate. If that was where Nick had gone, then she would go.

She rose into the air, ready to follow him even in death.

Nick darted through the trees and under the brush, using the cover to get as close to the buildings as possible. Jessie's scent was strong and fresh. She was here. He knew it.

He made a half circle of the property before halting.

The spread was impossibly large, with twelve cabins of various sizes scattered in the woods and one central mammoth log-construction lodge. Any of the buildings might have Jessie trapped inside.

Bess landed beside him.

"Nothing unusual from the air. Folks on a trail ride in the woods back there. I didn't see any guards."

Nick nodded. He had found Jessie's scent and set off again, keeping low and close to cover as he breathed in her familiar essence. He paused and pointed toward the large cabin.

"There?" asked Bess, landing on the ground at his left.

He nodded. She flapped her wings and flew around the log home. She perched on the deck and peered inside and then hopped over the roof and disappeared round back. Nick stole closer, making it under the porch before Bess returned.

"Curtains are all drawn. I can't see a thing. You have a plan?"

Nick transformed. "Kick in the damn door?"

"Without knowing how many there are?"

"Your suggestion?"

"Let me knock."

"No. If they are possessed, they will know what you are. We go together."

From somewhere beyond his vision came a startled female voice.

"Look! A buffalo!"

"Do you think it's tame?" asked another woman.

Bess hopped to the edge of their cover, with Nick close behind her. There, downwind, on the lawn stood a massive male buffalo. Nick recognized him instantly by his scent.

"Friend of yours?" asked Bess.

Nick assessed the sheer mass of the young bull, feeling better already. "Definitely."

Bess chortled. "Odds just got better."

The buffalo maintained his position, drawing a crowd. The distraction made it easy for Nick to transform back to a man and slip onto the porch.

The door was locked, so he lifted one of the rockers, constructed from sturdy logs, and threw it through the picture window. An instant later he dove through the void.

He came to his feet in a living room and was overwhelmed by the rank odor of death.

The room was still and unnaturally quiet. He followed Jessie's scent past the stone fireplace and the efficiency kitchen to the second bedroom at the back of the cabin. Light crept around the drawn navy blue blinds, giving the room in an eerie, melancholy mood.

It took only a moment to find her, lying on her side, unnaturally still, with her unfocused eyes staring out at nothing.

"Jessie!"

He reached her in an instant. Her skin was cool, as if she had just been dipped in ice water. The scent of death clung to her skin. He pressed his ear to her chest and listened. If not for his ability to hear faint sounds, he would have thought her dead, but her heart still did beat in a delayed cadence that could not keep her alive for long.

Jessie was dying.

Bess sailed into the room, landing on the floor beside him, and then surged upward to her full human height.

"What is wrong with her?" she asked, creeping closer.

"I don't know. She smells of death."

"Her aura is wrong. It is not that of a living soul, but she still has one, so she has not crossed." Bess leaned close. "I see Nagi's mark on her skin."

Nick growled. "He has done this to her."

Bess nodded. "A spirit wound."

Jessie's parents appeared in the doorway. Mrs. Healy gave a cry and pushed past Nick and Bess and attempted to lift her limp daughter from the bed.

"You've killed her."

"She's still alive," said Nick.

"Not for long," said Bess.

Mrs. Healy looked horrified.

"Can you reach her?" Nick asked Mrs. Healy.

"I've tried. She is behind some veil. She can't hear me and I can't understand what she is saying."

Bess straightened. "A veil? Does it shimmer like starlight?"

Mrs. Healy's grip on her daughter slackened as her mouth dropped open. "How did you know?"

Bess turned to Nick. "She has begun her journey on the Way of Souls."

Nick stood paralyzed. It was what Nagi had planned all along, to use Jessie in this way. Either Nick let Jessie die or he revealed the location of the Seer.

"He has sent her to the one place I cannot follow."

Mrs. Healy pressed her ear to Jessie's chest, then straightened in panic. "Do something!"

Nick scooped Jessie off the bed and turned to Bess. "If I don't bring her to Sebastian, she dies, and if I bring her, the Seer and her babies die."

Bess pressed a hand to Nick's shoulder. "Let me go to the Dream Walker. I can call her back."

"No time."

Bess stared up at Nick. "It's the only way to protect the Seer. Please, Nick."

Nick's heart was breaking. Jessie's cold, still body lay limp in his arms. He stared at Bess, silently begging her to help him. "All right."

"Keep her close. She has not crossed yet."

Nick sank to the bed, holding Jessie in his lap as he looked at Bess. "If you are too late, tell her I will not be far behind her."

Bess's dark eyes widened as she nodded. "Have courage, brother. I will be faster than the wind."

With that, Bess transformed into her raven self and shot out the door, crying her hoarse call of farewell. George followed her to the cabin door and watched her disappear into the clouds above them.

Bess found the Way of Souls with a speed born of experience and urgency. She followed the shimmering silver path of starlight, gliding over the river of souls to find Jessie. Nick's soul mate stood before Hihankara, the old crone who guarded the Spirit Road.

Bess had never seen this happen. Hihankara either let a soul pass or cast them from the Way of Souls. She never hesitated or wavered. She knew exactly who should cross and who should not. By the tattoos that appeared only after death.

Bess hovered in the air. "Hihankara, what happens here?"

It was the first time Bess had ever spoken to Hihankara. The guardian tolerated a raven flying over her road but did not like it. She thought it disrespectful to disturb the departed with the business of the living.

"This one does not have any tattoos at all," growled the old Spirit. "She cannot pass."

"You can't stop me. I *will* follow him," said Jessie.

"And I've told you, he did not cross."

"Who?" asked Bess.

"Nick. Nagi has killed him," said Jessie.

Bess understood Nagi's trick now. By making Jessie believe Nick had gone before her, he had fooled her into giving up.

"No. He's alive," said Bess.

Jessie jerked her head to look at Bess. "I don't understand."

"A trick," said Bess. "Nagi is using you to force Nick to call the Healer. He is about to reveal the Seer."

"What?"

"He is with you now. Can you not feel him?"

Jessie stared down at her empty hand and then back at Bess in wonderment. "Yes. I can."

An instant later her astral form rocketed away in a streak of silver too fast for even Bess to follow.

Hihankara grumbled, "No wonder she had no tattoos. The girl isn't even dead yet. Impudence!" She turned to Bess. "Did you say, Nagi?"

Bess's wings grew tired from hovering. "I did."

"He should not meddle with the living," said Hihankara, more to herself than Bess.

"I agree. But all is not as it should be. Farewell, wise one." With that she turned about and began the journey back to the world of the living. She raced, trying to reach her friends, knowing that Nagi had allowed Nick to find Jessie. But she doubted their escape would be so easy.

"My lord," said the ghost sentry to Nagi, "the wolf has arrived."

"Excellent. Has he found the Dream Walker?"

"Yes, Lord."

"And has he called the Healer?"

"Not yet, Lord."

"How long has he been with her?"

"Many minutes, Lord."

"Yet he sent no signal?" Would the wolf let the Dream Walker die rather than expose his friend? It was a course he did consider. To let a soul mate die... He couldn't believe it.

"What about the others, Lord?"

Nagi hesitated. "What others?"

"A raven, buffalo and two Niyanoka."

Nagi simmered. "The Dream Children are united with the Skinwalkers?"

The ghost did not answer. Caution, no doubt, kept him mum.

It was as he feared. "Who are the Niyanoka?"

"The Dream Walker's parents."

"Ah." Nagi understood temporary alliances that sprang from mutual interest. "Use as many as you need, but see none of them live to tell the tale."

"Yes, my lord."

The ghost departed, leaving Nagi to consider his plan. It was possible that all he would accomplish was the death of three Skinwalkers and the girl's parents. He had not considered that Skinwalkers would prove so selfless. It was maddening. Perhaps he had such low expectations because of the souls he normally judged. Still he was stronger than any of them.

The room about him went dark and he felt a presence.

"Nagi? What are you up to?"

He knew the voice. It was Hihankara.

"Why does the raven say you tricked a Dream Walker into walking before her time?"

Nagi shivered and dissolved back into the safety of his circle, leaving his ghosts to fight alone.

Chapter 24

Jessie held on to Nick's hand, feeling it with her body as her spirit returned to him. She opened her eyes to find him there beside her, whole and perfect, just as Bess had promised.

"You're alive," she whispered.

Nick smiled down at her, his eyes shimmering with emotion. "Because of you."

She reached for him and he pulled her gently into his lap, caressing her.

"I thought he had killed you, so I followed."

Nick nodded, his cheek moist against hers. "I know. But we're together now."

"Always," promised Jessie.

Her father's voice interrupted them. "Nick."

Jessie glanced about until she found her father, standing by the window, peering out past the blinds.

Beside him, her mother stood with folded arms, her eyes glittering with fury.

"I taught you the law. Yet you left the earthly plane. That was an incredibly dangerous thing to do."

Jessie stiffened at her mother's words and her face flushed, but she said nothing in her own defense.

"So you are bonded to him?" asked her mother.

Jessie tried to rise and found her body stiff and numb. Nick supported her as she stood unsteadily on her feet. How long had she been on the Spirit Road?

Nick kept one arm about her waist. She pressed her hand over his, gathering strength from his courage.

"Yes," she said.

Her mother pressed a hand to her forehead in despair, covering her eyes.

Tuff charged through the door in human form. "They're coming. We have to go now."

Nick helped Jessie to the door, where she froze and staggered backward. Outside the guests and employees of the ranch gathered, their ghostly yellow eyes turned toward the little cabin.

Above them came the cry of a raven as Bess soared over them, returning from her long journey to fight by their sides.

"This is bad," said George.

It *was* bad. Nick knew it, sensed it as he crossed the threshold of the cabin door. How could there be so many? Nick could not fathom the number advancing toward them. He knew that the only way for him to free a human from possession was to kill him. He felt sick at the prospect of killing so many innocents.

"Here they come," said George. He closed his eyes for a moment as he stepped back and then opened them again, staring out at the mob. He turned to Nick, looking worried. "My suggestions don't work on the possessed."

"Get back," said Nick.

George cleared the doorway just as three men barged in. Nick had time only to step in front of Jessie before they were on him.

The odor of death would have been enough to recognize them as possessed. But Nick could see the deathly yellow glow of their eyes.

They came at him all together and without weapons. It was a costly mistake. He threw the closest out the window. The second got one hand on Nick before Nick broke his arm. The man staggered away, howling in agony, his elbow bending backward at an unnatural angle. Nick ducked to avoid the swing from the youngest of the three and went for his legs, driving his shoulder into the man's stomach as he carried him backward. They hit the wide pine floorboards together and with enough force to knock the wind out of the man.

Tuff glanced out the door. "More coming. Best face them in the open."

Tuff stepped onto the porch. Nick followed, carrying Jessie, who was still barely able to stand. Beyond the gleaming varnish of the log rail, three dozen men and women, still as zombies, stood in a rough half circle surrounding the cabin. The stink of death made Nick gag. He lowered Jessie to his side, keeping her close, knowing he could not fight and protect her. She bore her own weight now but clung to his middle.

Her voice was hushed as she stared out at the army of possessed humans. "Oh, my God."

Nicholas judged the half dozen horse wranglers to be the biggest threat. They looked young and strong. The cowboys stood side by side with paunchy tourists who wore an odd assortment of sneakers, ball caps and new denim. One woman stood in a bikini and had bare feet, as if she'd just been summoned from the pool. Suntan lotion made her bare legs gleam in the sun.

They crept relentlessly, steadily forward, tightening the circle.

"We can't kill them," said Jessie. "It's my duty to preserve human life."

"We'll make a run for it. Try to reach the woods," said Nicholas.

He could smell Jessie's panic.

"There are so many."

He clasped her hand. "Get ready."

He didn't think they'd make it, but he would not retreat into the house. Better to fight on open ground than be trapped in the cabin.

The bellowing made him glance away from his foe for just an instant. Beside him, Tuff had taken his animal form. The horde before him made no indication that they heard the warning cry of the bull buffalo before it charged. The beast tossed its massive head as it plowed forward, knocking people aside like bowling pins. The bull cleared a furrow through the enemy; then it turned around, pawing the ground.

Nick needed no further invitation. He grabbed Jessie, tossed her over his shoulder and ran down the steps. Then he threw her up on the buffalo's back.

"Hold on," he shouted, then turned to the bull. "She's on, Tuff. Go! Go!"

The buffalo lowered its head and charged. Several of the humans managed to clutch at Jessie's legs, but Nick ran beside the bull, throwing off the humans who grabbed and tore at her. He retained the speed of his wolf self in human form and easily kept up with the buffalo. He heard Jessie's mother scream and turned to see George swinging his fist as the enemy overwhelmed them.

He turned back, throwing off the men and women that attacked her parents.

Behind him, Tuff bellowed. Nick saw him slow under the sheer number of people crowding, screaming, clawing. As Tuff knocked them away, more poured from the cabins, replacing the fallen. Cooks with knives appeared and valets, women who worked in the spa and at the front desk, their cheery country-style uniforms now a mocking aberration.

Nick saw there were too many, that they would lose. The humans who were seriously injured or unconscious lay useless as old snake skins as more unseen ghosts took possession of healthy hosts to manipulate.

The buffalo came to a standstill. Nick ran to Jessie, dragging her from Tuff's back. He curled about her, protecting her from the shower of blows with his body. Tuff stamped and circled, swinging his great horned head to drive back those he could.

Above them, Bess flapped and cried, helpless to defend her friends.

The winds increased to a roaring gale that knocked the people flat. Only Tuff retained his footing as the tornado touched down beyond the corral, scattering the horses.

The Thunderbirds had arrived, carrying help. Nick thought of all the Inanoka he had met and wondered who had responded to his urgent call.

The answer sent a shiver of dread down his body, for there in the clearing stood the great grizzly bear. Nick recognized him instantly.

Sebastian, the Healer, his best friend and the husband of the last Seer of Souls, had come.

But his wife? *Please,* thought Nicholas, *don't let her be here.*

He strained his neck to see. The winds lifted, and Sebastian roared and then fell to all fours, charging forward. And then he saw Michaela, running swiftly after her husband, her long braid bobbing behind her. She was slim and sleek again. How long ago had she delivered her twins?

The ghost army turned from him in unison, responding to some signal he could not hear. En masse, they charged the bear and the Seer, breaking through the wooden fence in the paddock.

Nicholas's heart sank. All his efforts to protect the last Seer of Souls had come to nothing. She had followed her husband, coming to rescue his miserable hide.

They would be killed.

And it would be his fault.

Nick saw the horses in the paddock now charging Sebastian. He called a warning.

Sebastian reared to attack the horses. Hooves flashed as the bear swung his massive arm. Beside him, his wife, Michaela, gripped a medicine wheel and chanted. The horses leaped back, trembled and then fell to their sides, kicking wildly.

"Go back," shouted Nick. "Call the winds."

They could not hear him, for they continued toward the army of howling ghosts. Behind them the horses rolled suddenly to their feet, kicking and bucking as they made their mad escape from the bear.

Sebastian moved to stand before his wife. He was mighty and brave. But Nick knew that even he could not win against such numbers.

Nick glanced at Jessie. She was flushed and shaken, but uninjured.

"Hurry," she urged. "Help them."

Nick ran toward his friends, pushing and shoving this mass of manipulated humanity as he passed. How many would he kill before they killed him?

Michaela raised her face to the wispy white clouds, holding the medicine wheel up to the sunshine. Her chanted song rose clear and true above the moan of the approaching horde. In unison the people halted, clamping their hands to their ears as if her lovely prayer was some heinous screeching. They dropped to their knees, still clutching their heads, and together collapsed on the ground.

Nick examined the fallen. They all lay in the same

direction, heads pointed north, lying motionless, as felled wheat.

He crouched down to stare at a woman. Her eyes were open but had rolled back in her head, making them a disconcerting white. Her muscles were rigid, as if some invisible current ran through her body.

Jessie ran to him, wrapping an arm about his waist. "What's happening?"

Nick glanced this way and that. He, Jessie, Michaela, Sebastian, Bess and Tuff, now in human form, and Jessie's parents were the only ones still standing.

"She did something to them," said Tuff, gazing with caution at Michaela. "What is her power?"

Nick smiled at Michaela, who lowered her wheel as he spoke to Tuff. "This is Michaela, the last Seer of Souls."

She shook her head, beaming a great smile. "Last no longer."

Nick's eyes widened as he remembered. Her infants were now in this world. Were they Seers, as well? It explained Nagi's impatience to kill her.

Sebastian transformed to human form and strode forward. He was a great mountain of a man with more height and brawn than Nick. He clasped Nick's forearm, using it to drag him forward for a hug so tight several of his ribs popped.

"Easy, bear, you'll crush the life out of me."

"I'm so glad to see you safe," said Sebastian, now thumping Nick on his shoulders in a steady rain of affectionate blows. "I got your distress call."

Nick grabbed his hands to still them. "I didn't want you to come."

"I know, but Michaela has learned a few tricks since you've seen her. Her father's been teaching her. She can send them for judgment now."

Sebastian seemed to only just notice Jessie. He released Nick, who tried not to sag with relief.

"So, this is the little Spirit Child who saved your life. We have heard of you." Sebastian grabbed Jessie about the waist and spun her in a circle. "Thank you."

Michaela reached her husband. "Put her down now. You're frightening her."

He did, his face reddening as he lowered her back to the ground. "Was I?" He leaned toward Jessie for confirmation.

"Well, maybe a little." She motioned toward the slim native man beside her. "This is Tuff. He fixed Nick's injuries."

Sebastian bowed to the buffalo. "Thank you, brother, for your sacrifice."

Tuff returned the bow. "It is my duty."

Michaela came forward and kissed Nick. "We're so happy you are all right."

It was then that the moaning began. All around the injured humans began to cry out in pain and confusion. The ground, once as still as a graveyard, now undulated with writhing humanity.

Nick shook his head, suddenly at a loss. "How could there be so many?"

Michaela answered. "Nagi has not been collecting the evil souls who refuse to walk the Spirit Road upon their death. Or, rather, he has been collecting them, but instead of taking them to his circle, he has recruited for his earthbound army."

"Great Spirit save us," whispered Jessie.

The wounded continued to call for help, while the uninjured sat up, shaking their heads in bewilderment.

Tuff surveyed the scene. "There are many here in need of help."

Sebastian rested a hand on him. "We can manage it together."

Jessie gaped at the fallen army. "But what about our oath to keep our world secret? They've already seen too much."

Her father interrupted. "I can help with that."

They turned to see Jessie's parents hurrying forward. Nick recalled that her father had the gift of suggestion. But to influence so many, was it even possible?

Jessie swayed and Nick caught her.

"What's wrong?"

"I've been out of my body so long, I'm just…"

"Exhausted," finished her mother, slipping her arm about Jessie's waist. "That's why we set limits. It's bad for the body to be alone so long."

Nick retained his hold on Jessie's shoulders, ready to engage in a tug-of-war with her mother.

Mrs. Healy fixed her cold stare on him. "I know how to care for her. Do you?"

Uncertainty stirred in him and he looked to Jessie.

"It's all right. I'll just be in the lodge, waiting for you," she said.

"I'll come along."

"You have to protect the Seer. Make sure she and Sebastian get away safely."

Nick knew she was right and let his grip relax, but only enough to capture her hand. He trusted her, but he did not trust her parents.

"Please," whispered Jessie, swaying.

The exhaustion in her face convinced him. He released her. "I'll be quick."

She nodded wearily as her mother guided her away.

Her father paused in the center of the men and women, now rising from the grassy lawn.

"Folks, I think you'll all want to gather around me now. You'll want to hear this."

They did. Everyone who could stand now followed this pied piper as he led them toward the lodge. It made separating the injured an easy matter.

"We're all going into the lodge for a meeting and we'll fill you in on this crazy weather. Boy, I'll bet you all feel lucky to have safely come through it. I know you admire the way the staff protected you from injury. Quick thinking on their part to get you out of those buildings."

Nick watched in wonder as the men and women nodded their heads in agreement with his version of events.

"They won't remember the possession," said Michaela. "That will just be a blank spot. It's good to have someone fill in the pieces, even if they aren't the actual ones that happened. I take it he's a Peacemaker."

Nick nodded. "So he said."

He turned to the injured, assisting Sebastian and Tuff as they assessed the damage from the battle. Together the bear and buffalo began the process of restoring the injured.

Michaela watched over her husband and scanned the area like a soldier on patrol.

Nicholas came to stand beside her, guarding her as his friend did his work.

"Is it really safe for you here?"

Bess landed on a fence post, listening to them with her bright eyes twinkling.

"I've sent all the ghosts away," Bess said.

Tension remained in Michaela's shoulders and her attention continued to wander over the open area.

Bess flapped her wings. "But they will all be arriving in the Circle of Ghosts together. These souls will surely draw Nagi's notice."

Michaela nodded. "It's a risk."

Bess's neck cowl lifted as a measure of her unease.

"You can't be here," said Nicholas.

"But here I stay, until my husband has finished his work."

Nick glanced at Sebastian. "It is not his duty to protect men."

"But it is mine," she answered. "And I am his and so it falls to him, as well."

Bess piped up. "The buffalo can treat them."

Michaela shook her head in resignation. "So many are injured and so seriously, the effort would kill him. Buffalos are strong, but no living creature could endure such pain."

Nicholas pressed his lips together. He would trade all these lives for hers. She was necessary, vital to their fight against Nagi.

She lay a hand on his arm for just a moment. "He will be quick," she assured.

Nick glanced toward the lodge, wondering if Jessie was all right without him.

Michaela's voice intruded into his thoughts. "And then you can return to her."

He flushed and nodded.

The Seer gave him an assessing look. "Nicholas, this Dream Walker saved your life and defies her parents for you."

"Yes," he said, reluctant as always to reveal his feelings.

She waited until it was clear he would say nothing further and then she smiled. "You're worse than Sebastian. How do you feel about her?"

He met Michaela's gaze, seeing nothing but her sweet serenity and compassion.

"I love her," he admitted. "She is my soul mate."

Michaela clapped her hands together and then threw her arms about Nick. "Oh, I'm so happy for you both."

Nick dragged Michaela's hands from about his neck and returned his attention to scanning for potential threats, searching for ghosts that he knew he could not see. But if one possessed being came near, he could smell it.

"I can't wait to tell Sebastian. He'll be over the moon."

Nick thought his friend would have a field day and

already dreaded the comments he felt sure would come his way. He'd been a bachelor for nearly a century and never had a steady relationship in all that time.

He stayed by his friend's wife as Sebastian worked. Tuff grew weak from his efforts but continued on without complaint. Nick had never seen so stalwart a Skinwalker. His sacrifice humbled him again. Tuff gave this gift to strangers, selflessly.

When he tried to heal the horse, Sebastian stepped in. "Rest, brother. You have finished your work."

Tuff nodded his acceptance. He looked near collapse. Nicholas slipped an arm around him and felt him trembling. He knew he should bring him to the lodge and give him some food and water, but he could not leave Michaela and Sebastian. So, he moved Tuff only as far as the bench beside the barn, where he could rest in the shade.

Michaela directed the recovered people to the lodge, where Jessie's father could work his gift.

Nick glanced toward Sebastian, who chanted over the last of the injured guests. He had to hurry. Any moment Nagi might discover that his forces had been defeated.

Chapter 25

The number of souls rushing into his circle was not startling, but the sheer blackness of these arrivals did confound Nagi.

Such happenings could mean many things, but the worst possibility overshadowed the rest. The Seer had learned to use her gift.

Somewhere high above him the old hag Hihankara had measured each soul and found them lacking. Had she reported the unusual influx of evil to the Spirit World? The old crone was already suspicious.

Nagi felt a moment's worry. It was too soon. He had chosen not to use the countless ghosts here in his circle in order to avoid notice. It was the very reason he had chosen only the earth-bound ghosts for his army.

He was no fool, after all. It was one thing to fight Halflings and Supernaturals, but quite another to face a true Spirit with powers equal to or greater than his own. He hoped to possess the earth before the others learned of his territorial expansion.

He needed to know what happened. He called the fallen hundred-odd souls from their march. These were the uncollected ghosts he had purposefully overlooked—his light cavalry, his vanguard. Among them were the very three who had captured the little Dream Walker in order to use her against the wolf. Had the Seer escaped? Had not one in his army endured to follow the bear?

He gathered their stories. The Seer had emerged, fought and won. She had learned the secrets of sending souls for judgment. How many had she defeated?

She would be weakened by such an ordeal, like a warrior after the Sun Dance. It gave him another chance to seize her. He knew where she had been very recently. If she was wise, she would have already fled.

Had she fought while carrying her children or—his mind curled about another possibility—had she birthed them? That would only add to her weakness. The twins, the two prophesized great Seers, might at this very minute be helpless and unprotected. Perhaps a victory could be forged from this loss.

Nagi rose through the heavens, making his way swiftly to the place where his battle had been waged to see if any were foolish enough to linger.

Sebastian finished healing the last of the guests at the J Bar M Dude Ranch and helped Tuff heal, as well.

"You must go, brother," said Nick to Sebastian.

"Yes."

Tuff stretched, looking well but tired. "I have a truck. I'll take you where you and your wife would like to go."

Sebastian smiled and clasped his hand down on Tuff's shoulder in thanks. Nick was impressed that Tuff did not move in the slightest at the contact.

"We'd appreciate it."

Tuff led the way and held open the door for Michaela as Sebastian assisted his wife. Michaela hesitated and glanced at Sebastian.

"Have you asked Nick yet?"

Sebastian shook his head. "I was hoping to find them together."

Michaela's smile faded a little. "No time for that now." She turned to Nick and waited for Sebastian to speak.

Sebastian grinned at him. "Nicholas, we want you and Jessie to name our children."

Nick gasped at the request. The naming of infants was usually reserved for a family member. To be chosen for the naming ceremony was the greatest honor.

Nick straightened, feeling somehow a little taller as he nodded, accepting the responsibility. It took him another moment to find his voice. "Yes, brother. I'd be honored."

Sebastian smiled. "And Jessie?"

"I will tell her that it is your wish for her to take part."

"The ceremony is in three weeks, on the new moon. We will expect you then." Michaela kissed Nick. "Take good care of my sister and hurry from this place before Nagi discovers what has become of his warriors."

Nick and Sebastian clasped forearms. "Is it safe for us to come?" Nick asked.

"Michaela thinks so."

Michaela smiled. "Any ghost that follows you will be sorry, for I will send them to judgment."

"And Nagi?"

Sebastian and Michaela exchanged looks. "There are always the Thunderbirds."

"I would not bring harm to you or yours."

Sebastian nodded. "Then come to us soon."

They broke apart and Sebastian helped Michaela into the truck. Nick clasped Tuff's hand and thanked him once more, and then Tuff started the engine. In a moment they were waving through the glass as Tuff drove them north.

Nick felt alone once more. He tried not to let the feeling bite deep; he had grown used to isolation, believing there was no other path for him. Now Jessie gave him hope that things might be different. But first he must face Jessie's parents and get them safely away. Perhaps the most difficult battle still lay ahead.

Bess fluttered down to land at Nick's feet and then rose as she shifted to her human form, her feather cloak changing almost instantaneously into a rather short black dress and calf-clinging boots with high heels that made her nearly as tall as he was.

It was the kind of outfit that he would have found appealing before he'd met Jessie.

"Time to go," Bess said. Her eyes flashed playfully as she stepped up to clasp his arm.

He said nothing, but somehow she sensed the difference and her smile died.

She arched an eyebrow at him. "Not done playing house?"

"It's not a game."

Her hand slipped from his arm. "She's not like us. She won't understand you." Bess's gaze challenged him as she stood stiffly before him, holding herself ready for the rejection she sensed was to come. He had never meant to hurt her. Their few times together had been born more of the loneliness of their solitary existence than any real attraction.

"She will grow to understand."

"I should have left her on the Way of Souls."

Nick felt the fiery urge to defend Jessie but held his control. "You do not understand how it is with us."

"Don't I?" Bess turned her back on him. "Just don't call me when you get bored."

He rested a hand on her shoulder, feeling again the smooth, firm skin at the juncture of her neck. She turned toward him, hope blossoming in her eyes.

"Bess..." He met her stare. "She's my soul mate."

Bess stepped from his grip. "That one?" Shock echoed in her voice.

For a moment he thought she might cry, but instead she gathered herself like a warrior before battle.

"She doesn't deserve you."

"I'm sorry, Bess."

Her eyes flashed. "Don't be. I am used to my own company."

Nick took another step in her direction and she halted him with an uplifted hand.

Her eyes glittered luminescent. The sight punched him in the gut. "If Sebastian and I both have found mates, than you may also."

She huffed. "That would relieve your conscience, no doubt." She aimed a finger at him. "Don't you dare pity me, wolf. I did not give anything I did not get." She hesitated, as if she would say more.

"Bess, we are still friends, aren't we?" He had few enough that he could rely on and could ill afford to lose one.

She gave him a look of infinite sadness. "In time, perhaps."

With that she lifted her arms and shifted into the large glossy raven, rising up into the endless blue sky.

He watched her solitary ascent remembering how it felt to be that alone.

Nick headed toward the lodge at a jog. He needed to get Jessie and her family away from here before Nagi appeared.

He hurried through the massive double doors and past the reception area to the lobby beyond. The great hall was flooded with light from the windows that reached the peak of the roofline. The room was divided only by furniture, which was arranged to create a central foyer before a rustic staircase. To the left, couches and chairs, upholstered with cowhide, circled a massive fieldstone fireplace. To the right, Jessie's father spoke to the recovering victims who were seated on benches before long pine tables in the dining area.

"That was a bad fall you took in the barn. Lucky you didn't break anything."

The portly man nodded.

"Maybe you want to soak in the hot tub this afternoon."

The man heaved himself up and waddled off.

George worked methodically, moving from one group to the next until all the people had acceptable explanations for their lingering ailments.

Nick followed Jessie's scent through the room, but George stepped before him.

"Well, that was good work. We are finished up now. Time for you to get going."

Nick shook his head. "Where is Jessie?"

"She's not coming with you," said George.

Nick growled and stepped forward. George, to his credit, did not retreat.

"She doesn't want to see you."

Nick gave him a smile that was more a baring of teeth. "She'll have to tell me that herself."

"She's been in danger every minute since she met you. It's best for you both if you'd end this now."

"I'm going to see her."

"Haven't you caused her enough pain? Do you really want to make her an outcast, too? You will cost her everything." George's voice changed. It became soothing and the cadence was deeply appealing. "She's been through a lot. Her mother is with her. We'll take care of her from here."

Nick hesitated. "I want to see her."

"No, you don't."

Nick's eyes narrowed as he tried to hold on to his own thoughts.

"You love her too much to put her in danger. She's safest with us. If you love her, you'll let her go."

Nicholas felt the pressing burden of guilt. Still, he glanced toward the back of the lodge, drawn by the trail of Jessie's familiar scent.

"Nicholas, look at me." Her father's voice called him back. "She's safe with her family. Your work is elsewhere. You need to protect the Seer."

Nicholas nodded and then straightened as his own thoughts flooded past the ones George had fed him. George was doing to him what he had done to all these people. The only difference was that his words were true.

"Let me pass, George."

"No," he said, his voice adamant and cold.

It would have been an easy matter to defeat him, but instead, Nick chose to simply push past him.

George was left to run to catch Nick as he charged down a long hallway.

Jessie's sweet essence filled his nostrils as he ran along a narrow corridor with hotel rooms flanking either side. He paused at a door, knowing she lay beyond.

"Jessie?"

Her voice, sounded hopeful. "Nicholas?"

Then came another female voice, hard, angry—her mother. "Go away, wolf."

He tried the door and found it bolted. Beyond it, he recognized the whisper of footsteps on carpet.

"Let go of me, Mom."

Nick gripped the handle, found it locked and prepared to throw his shoulder against the door. But the lock clicked open and Jessie appeared in the gap.

Her cheeks were pink, her hair disheveled, but somehow she managed to give him a smile.

Her mother stood behind her, lips pressed in disapproval. Her father caught up, his stride purposeful as his heels pounded the native-motif carpeting.

She was his soul mate, his one true love. Yet to accept him, she must give up her family, friends, community— everything. It wasn't right to ask her, to beg her to choose him. Still, he stood there like a whipped dog, holding out his heart to her.

"Jessie," he whispered, "come with me."

Chapter 26

Jessie's limbs still trembled and pain stabbed behind her eyes, both remnants of her extended journey out of body. But she straightened to face her mother and father, who stood side by side in a unified front. They had raised her to be Niyanoka and expected her to bring them honor by walking the Red Road. She did not go with them and so she must prepare herself that they would cease to recognize her as their daughter.

She turned her head. There stood Nick, solitary as he had always been, the eternal outsider, who saw in her a chance to belong. He wanted her to walk at his side through the centuries and be what she'd been born to be, his soul mate.

She saw the cautious hunch of his powerful shoulders and the alert watchfulness of his eyes. Even in human form, he was ever the wolf. He stared boldly at her, urging her to have the courage to come to him.

She took one step, a tiny step, yet the biggest of her life. Right there in the hotel corridor, she moved from her parents to stand beside Nicholas.

He wrapped one arm around her, pulling her tight, protecting her from the approaching firestorm. She felt bathed in his willingness to defend her but found she did not need it.

"Jessica Elizabeth! You come over here this instant." Her mother billowed like a volcano about to blow, her face brightening to a lava red.

Her father tried a different tack. "Come here, pump-kin."

She shook her head. "Not this time."

Her parents exchanged a long look and then faced her again like a tag team in a wrestling match.

"What will our friends say?" said her mother, going for guilt. "For goodness' sake, Jessica, think of someone besides yourself for once."

Was it selfish to love this man? Perhaps, but no less so than to expect one's daughter to give up her one true love so she would not embarrass you. They were her parents. It was her duty to do them honor. But they did not have the right to choose her path.

Her mother waited for her answer. If she wanted an apology, she'd have a long wait. Jessie refused to beg forgiveness for the best thing that had ever happened to her. And she would not ask permission to take what was hers.

"Jessica?"

Nick felt the muscles in Jessie's back contract, as if she was prepared to fight, and instantly saw why. Nick glanced from Jessie's face to see George raising his fist to throw a punch.

If it came to a fight, he knew who the victor would be. He hesitated only because he did not know how Jessie would take him pummeling her father. Even a victory would be a defeat.

Jessie's intention came clearly to Nick and he deferred to her, allowing her to step forward, only because he was certain she was in no danger.

Jessica sprang between her father and Nick aiming a finger at his nose.

"Don't you dare," she said to her father. "Don't you touch one hair on his head, or I will never speak to you again as long as I live."

Her father's mouth rounded in shock. Her mother gasped.

"How dare you dictate to us!" said Mrs. Healy.

Marta Healy cast an uncertain glance at her husband. If she had planned to threaten to disown her wayward daughter, Jessie had just cut the wind from her sails.

Nick could not keep his mouth from twitching in delight. His little Dream Walker was magnificent when she was angry. He had never had anyone come to *his* defense before.

After her father closed his gaping mouth, he stepped back. His wife linked elbows with him.

Jessie had taken their power from them. In that instant, her position had shifted from subordinate to equal.

Nick saw her as he had never seen her before, ferocious and protective, with fists bunched at her side, chin raised and body ready for battle. His woman was an alpha at last.

Nick could not keep himself from grinning, while Jessie stayed stern and aggressive as any pack leader.

"We'll keep this secret," said her father, "until you come to your senses."

Nick stiffened at this insult. But before he could speak, Jessie came to his defense again.

"Then we won't expect you at the wedding."

"Wedding!" screeched her mother.

"If he'll have me, yes."

Her mother extended a consolatory hand. "But, darling, be reasonable."

"I was ready to follow him on the Way of Souls. Do you think your disapproval will change my love for him? It will hurt me. But I can live without it."

It was true, Nick realized. She had walked the Way of Souls to reach him. He could hardly believe the tenacity of his mate. She was more courageous than any woman he had ever met and he was proud to call her his own.

"But he's dangerous. Nagi is after him. If he loves you, he won't put you in danger."

Nick ground his teeth at the realization that Marta Healy was right.

"It is just another reason he needs me. We're all in danger. You, me, them. Nagi is using humans. Doesn't that make it our fight?"

Her parents glanced at one another but said nothing.

"Mom, Dad, there is a battle coming, a war. We'll

need everyone. If the Niyanoka *and* Inanoka come together, we can win. Join us, please."

Her parents stared at the floor.

Jessie saw their unwillingness to change, even after all they had witnessed.

"You saw the ghosts," she said.

"It does not change our past," said Marta Healy, still glaring at Nick.

"I hope one day you will reconsider. I'll wait for that day."

Jessie hesitated, but her parents did not move or look up. They seemed embarrassed or perhaps they were already mourning losing her. Nick hoped their stubbornness did not keep them forever separated from their only daughter. From his perspective, the loss would be largely theirs.

He paused. "You should go now. Before Nagi returns."

The couple exchanged nervous looks and George tugged Marta past them.

Jessie glanced at Nick, her eyes steady. He extended his hand and she clasped it. The connection brought all her emotions to him. He felt her love and her sorrow and her pride. Pride? Yes, she was proud of him, proud to be with him and a part of him.

He smiled in wonder. "I can't believe it."

"But you should," said Jessie, squeezing his hand and leading them down the hall.

Jessie looked at her parents, scuttling out of sight. Nick was possessed by the sudden wave of grief she felt. It hit with such force he tripped. He did not dare stop, but clasped her hand, bringing her attention back to him and to the way out.

She stared at him and he nodded.

"I love you, too," she whispered.

They reached the lobby and paused. Visitors sat in chairs by the fireplace, with blackened eyes and broken arms, but they seemed oblivious to the large number of injured among them. The woman at the counter waved at them as they passed.

"You have a great day!" Her smile caused her split lip to bleed and she dabbed it with a colorful red bandanna.

Nick waved.

Outside, Jessie and Nick saw her parents climb stiffly into their car and start the engine. Apparently George had used L.J. gift to have someone retrieve his car from the road. They did not toot or wave as they pulled out.

Jessie watched them drive away, certain that her mother would not forgive her.

"Perhaps time will change them," said Nick.

"How did you do that? We aren't even touching."

"That one I read on your face."

"Do you think they will be all right? I mean, with Nagi after us?"

"There is no reason to follow them."

He left the rest unsaid. Her parents would have no contact with her and so they were in no danger.

They used the ranch van to bring them to Nick's rental. Nick held open the door to the red Mustang convertible. Jessie tried not to let him see the bone weariness she felt, but could not stifle the groan of exhaustion as she crawled into the leather seat. Nick hopped behind the wheel and lowered the top.

Jessie glanced about. "Where are the others?"

"Safely away, I hope."

Above them came the caw of a raven. Jessie shaded her eyes to look up at Bess in her bird form soaring in lazy circles.

"Will she say goodbye?"

Nick shook his head. "She never does."

The light hurt Jessie's eyes, another lingering effect of her long journey.

Jessie knew Nick loved her but the prickly thorn of jealousy still stabbed at her.

"Will you see her again?"

Nick took his gaze from the sky and studied Jessie before answering. "Not in the way you imply."

Jessie pressed her lips together to keep from revealing more of her insecurities.

"She does not threaten us. That time was born of loneliness, not love. I am grateful that I no longer walk that road."

He stroked her cheek. The wave of emotions caused her to sway. She felt the gnawing ache of loneliness he had carried for so long and the isolation known only to Skinwalkers. He had no community to foster him, no tribe, no true love. Only his friends and he was selective with them. He did not love Bess. Never had.

"How did you bear it?" she whispered.

He drew back to spare her his emotions.

Nick's smile held a deep sadness to it. "What choice did I have?"

Jessie glanced at the blue sky, following Bess's endless circle. "Only a true friend would have come to me on that road and turned me back."

Nick kept his thoughts to himself for the moment.

"Why did you do it?" he asked at last.

"What? Believe Nagi?"

"No." He turned to her. "Take the Way of Souls?"

"That's easy. I belong beside you no matter where you are. There is no other way for me now."

"Yet I feared your parents would turn you against me."

Jessie chuckled. "Nick, facing death can be a whole lot easier than facing down your mother."

He cocked his head in confusion, as if trying to determine if she was serious. She was.

"Your relationships are very complex."

She laughed at that. "I'll say."

Nick started the car and pulled out, lifting the top to shield them from the increasing wind. Jessie nestled in the seat beside him, happy to be alone with him at last.

She had none of the confusion or torment of their earlier time together. She had made her choice and was content for the first time since she could not remember when. She was safe. She was with Nick and the world seemed full of possibilities. The relief was palpable, pulsing like a heartbeat within her.

"Where are we going?" she asked.

Nick steered the car onto the main highway. "I can't

take you home. I'm sorry, Jess. But if he's trying to find us, he'll send a sentry there."

"How do you know?"

"It's what I'd do."

She couldn't go home. After all the losses, she had lost that, too.

He brushed her cheek and then drew back as if her thoughts had scalded him.

"Nick—"

"It's all right." He accelerated down the narrow road.

Jessie stared out the window at the golden grass and blue hills. She couldn't go home. But what was her home? She and her parents never stayed anywhere long. Her home was where they were, where her people were. But now all that had changed. Now her home was with Nick and she found that was exactly what she wanted most.

She glanced over at him and found him staring fixedly at the road, gripping the wheel a little too tightly.

What could she say to reassure him?

"Nick?"

"Jessie. You need to rest. You're exhausted."

She blinked at him, knowing he was right.

"We'll talk later," he promised.

The stress of the kidnapping and the battle fell upon her and she could not seem to keep her eyes open.

"Are you all right?" she muttered to Nick.

"Sleep. I'll protect you."

She knew he would. She let her eyes drift shut and did not open them until she felt the car stop. She was jarred awake, sitting up and glancing about. It was night and they sat under fluorescent lights beneath some kind of underpass.

"Easy," said Nick. "We're at a hotel."

Jessie rubbed her eyes and stretched as Nick held the door, then turned over the keys to the valet.

"Luggage, sir?" asked a man whose face seemed to pivot around a huge bushy gray mustache.

"No," said Nick.

Together they negotiated the lobby and reception desk, where Nick secured a suite. It was not until they were alone in the elevator that she noticed the tension rippling from Nick. Instinctively, she reached for him.

He stepped away. "Not yet."

It frightened her, this need to keep his thoughts and emotions locked up tight within himself. What was so terrible that he did not want her to know?

She knew he loved her, but was love enough for him, this loner who had never stayed in one place or with one woman for more than a few days? She knew what she wanted—never to leave his side. But what did Nick want? To have her with him always? It was a great change for him. Uncertainty made her heart trip along, steadily increasing into panic.

The elevator doors slid open, and he waited for her to precede him and then followed her to their suite, sliding the plastic key into the slot and waiting for the green light.

They found the large room dark. Nick seemed to have no trouble negotiating the room, for he swept past her.

A moment later she heard him click on the tall reading light by the upholstered chair.

She was afraid again, not of him, but of what he might say.

Nagi arrived at the sight of the battle to see not one of his ghosts remaining to meet him. All had been repelled by the Seer and sent for judgment. The Spirit Children and Skinwalkers had fled before his coming. Worse still, the Dream Walker had managed to heal the Spirit Wound by breaking free of the illusion of her mind. This meant she left no easy trail by which to lead him.

It was left only to decide how best to act.

The Seer might already have born her brats. Nagi finished his survey of the humans at their meaningless lives but found nothing of interest. He was preparing to depart when he chanced to glance skyward and caught sight of a tiny black speck high in the air.

His mind stretched back to the day his ghosts nearly killed the Seer. It was before she carried the babies. His ghosts had reported seeing a raven.

Could it be a Skinwalker? Nagi rose, light as a cloud of mist as he swept after the fast-flying bird.

Nick wished he could comfort Jessie, but to touch her was to let her see the heartache he carried in his soul. He had not meant to cause her such pain, or make her choose between him and the people she loved most in the world.

She had sacrificed her family, community and now her home, for him. She would never again see the horses that she dearly loved and he wondered if she would ever forgive him for it. If this soul-mate connection was such a gift, why had it nearly cost her life? When was the price too high? When did the weight of the losses kill the love you shared?

He wanted what was best for her. He just did not know if he was best. Before he met her, she had meaningful work, a home, a family; she was happy and safe. Now she was standing alone in a hotel room with only the clothes on her back.

How could she love him?

He feared it was like a thorn buried deep below the skin. After the prick, the festering began, until the infection poisoned the blood.

"Nick, please, you're frightening me."

"Jessie, I've lived alone for many years."

Her eyes grew round and her face went pale. But he continued.

"I never had to consider what was best for anyone but myself. Now I have you and I'm not sure what to do."

"What do you mean, not sure? You're my soul mate. We belong together." She stepped forward, hands extended.

"How can you forgive me?"

Her brow furrowed. "Forgive you? For what?"

"I've cost you everything."

"Nick, I love them, but they are wrong about you and about all Skinwalkers. I left because—"

"Because of me."

"No, that's not right. I left because they cannot accept

you, so they cannot accept me. This is the choice *they* made. It has nothing to do with us."

"Everything to do with us."

"Nick, I can't go back to things as they were. I've changed. I see the world differently and I see myself with you."

He felt his heart clench, wishing he could believe her. Wishing his love brought her joy instead of sorrow. Wanting so much to come in from the cold and find a place where he was welcome, where he belonged.

Still he wondered if she was better off without him.

Jessie's eyes narrowed and then one eyebrow cocked, as if she had just had some realization.

"Don't you even think about sacrificing our love to please them."

"The price is so high."

Her smile was sultry as she approached him. "I'll pay it, because I have gained everything, more than I deserve, in you."

Nick's breath caught at the honesty in her gaze.

"I'll fight them all to keep you," she said. "And I'll fight you, too, if I have to. No one is taking you from me. Not in this life or the next."

In his time upon the earth, many women had tried to possess him. But he had never loved, never trusted another soul with something as fragile as his heart. Now he realized that her words were true. He was holding back, not only to protect her, but to protect that part of himself that he had never given to anyone.

He raked his fingers through his hair. "I've been

alone so long. It's hard to believe you want me or that I can make you happy."

"Not so hard." She extended her arm. "Just take my hand."

He stared at her open palm and slowly threaded his fingers with hers. Jessie drew their clasped hands over her heart and closed her eyes.

At her touch, his fears and uncertainties drained away like sand through a sieve. This was his place, the one true belonging he thought he'd never find in this lifetime.

He was blessed by this holy bond. She loved him. He could feel it now. She did not blame or regret. She was happy and ready to stand beside him through any challenge. Her love was fierce and that she would fight any challengers and surmount any obstacle that kept her from him. And even so, her love was a gentle breeze that would caress him and accept him regardless of his faults.

He leaned forward, pressing his forehead to hers. "Can it be true?"

She wrapped her free hand about his middle. "It is true, wolf. You have finally met your match."

"And I thank the Great Mystery for it."

He lowered his head to kiss her and she lifted her mouth to meet him, giving him a sweet blending of yielding flesh and urgency.

Her tongue darted into his mouth, firing a desire so bright that he knew it would burn for centuries.

Epilogue

Sun streamed down through the leafy canopy above them as the gathering stood in a sacred circle around the small glowing fire.

Jessie stood beside Nick and beside him stood the parents of the twins, Sebastian and Michaela. Sebastian wore his bearskin cloak over traditional buckskin attire and Michaela was radiant in a heavily beaded white deerskin dress. About her neck hung a small medicine wheel. Michaela held her daughter and Sebastian cradled his son. Both infants were naked except for the swaddling of bearskin.

Finishing their circle was Tuff. He stood in a medicine shirt, dyed green and heavily adorned with long strands of buffalo hair tied across the chest.

In one hand he held a bundle of smoldering dried sage. He waved the other hand rhythmically through the cleansing sacred smoke, passing it over the babies pink bodies, blessing them.

"We welcome these souls to the physical world and thank them for the courage it takes to walk the Red Road that is this earthly life."

Jessie grew nervous about her part in the ceremony. She and Nick had spent several days with the babies, in an effort to choose names that would serve them best. Jessie had even visited their dreams and had found this time together most revealing.

The infants had asked her for two names. One rooted in the traditions of their people to remind them of where they came from and one common name to allow them to walk more easily in the white world. Their first name would be known only by their family and the other would be offered to outsiders.

Jessie hoped she and Nick had chosen wisely and wondered if the parents would be pleased. She glanced nervously at Nick. He met her gaze and his eyes narrowed almost imperceptibly, as if he was trying to gauge her thoughts. Then he gave up and captured her hand. Immediately, she felt his calm reassurance flow to her. He had concealed none of the turmoil billowing inside her and felt completely at ease both in the forest and with their decision.

As she fretted, he dreamed. His thoughts flowed to her like a strong current in the ocean. He marveled at these two infants, the firstborn of their two races. But primarily he wondered if together he and Jessie might add to their numbers.

Her eyes widened and she stared at him. His smile was devilish and his eyes glittered with promise.

He leaned close to her and whispered into her ear. "I hope the next ceremony will welcome our child to this world."

Jessie could not keep from glowing with hope at his wish.

Beside her, Tuff seemed in his element as he chanted in Lakota. Jessie knew this language and was happy she could understand his words, for she thought she had never heard a more lovely prayer.

Into our midst comes new life.
We welcome you to this world of light.
Here you will find belonging and respect among
your own.
Your mother and father will protect you until the
wheel
turns round and it is your time to protect them.
And so the circle forever spins.
May the Great Spirit watch over you
as you walk your path.
Walk in beauty.
*Mitakuye Oyasin.**

Tuff's voice was low and sweet and resonant. Jessie stood close to Nick, who draped his arm about her.

Jessie found herself smiling at the prayer as she stared down at the infants. These children would carry a grave responsibility for they must protect both those who walk on two legs and those who walk on four. She hoped their path would be smooth.

Nick leaned in. "They have not come for an easy journey. These two have come because they are needed."

She was not startled that he knew her thoughts. She had become accustomed to this bond. It was a comfort and a wonder to her.

Michaela offered her baby girl to Jessie with the bright smile of a proud mother. Jessie cradled the infant to her breast and waited as Nicholas accepted the boy child from Sebastian. Jessie was not surprised to see the tears shimmering in the great bear's eyes. Though even in human form he was huge and mighty, here he was still vulnerable as any new father, hopeful that his children would be happy on this earth.

She knew he wondered if they would be Skinwalkers like him or Seers like his wife. They had spoken at length and at last decided that only time would reveal what would come.

Sebastian spoke to his son first. "I welcome you to our family and give you this necklace as a reminder that you are of the Bear Clan and will always be a part of me." He slipped the necklace over his son's head. It looked enormous on the baby, who tried unsuccessfully to grasp the new trinket. Sebastian turned to his daughter and offered her a similar gift. "I offer you this gift from the earth, so you will know always where you come from and that you are loved."

Jessie shifted her charge to allow Sebastian to slip the long bear-claw pendant over the baby's head.

Tuff shook a rattle and Jessie and Nick faced him.

"What name do you give to this child, Gray Hunter?" asked Tuff.

Jessie stared in surprise, having never heard Nick's given name.

"He is to be Dances with Moonlight."

Tuff smiled and used his thumb to smudge red earth onto the boy's forehead. "Welcome, Dances with Moonlight."

He turned next to Jessie. "How will this one be called?"

"She is to be Night Sky Woman in honor of her birth beneath the stars."

Tuff repeated the smudge on the girl. "Welcome, Night Sky Woman."

He turned to Michaela. "How will they be called by those outside the family?"

"My son is Blake," said Michaela. "And my daughter is Samantha."

Tuff shook his rattle to the sky.

"Sun, moon and stars, make welcome these new souls who walk the earth and follow the Red Road."

* * * * *

---

* *Mitakuye Oyasin* is Lakota for "All my relations included." It is traditionally used as a closing for a blessing to indicate that all things are connected.

Terminology

DREAM WALKER*: A NIYANOKA with the ability to visit another person's dreams and work mental and/or physical healing during the visitation. The human visited has no memory of the visit.

CIRCLE OF GHOSTS: The final home of all ghosts who once led evil lives and are punished when HIHANKARA pushes them from the SPIRIT ROAD into the circle, where they drift for eternity in endless circles. This ghostly prison is presided over by NAGI. Some ghosts are eventually released from this prison by the prayers of those who live a pure life.

GHOST: The remains of humans after they have left their earthly vessels.

HALFLING: Any creature with one SPIRIT and one HUMAN parent.

HANWI: The moon is a reflective female SPIRIT who warms MAKA when the WI is absent.

HEYOKA: A SPIRIT of chaos who is a double-faced SPIRIT with a split personality and emotions. He represents joy and sorrow, war and peace and all other opposites. Humans who see WAKINYAN (THUNDERBEINGS) become living HEYYOKAS and do the opposite of what is expected.

HIHANKARA: The crone who guards the SPIRIT ROAD. If the soul has walked the RED ROAD and has led a righteous life it bears the proper tattoos and is allowed to pass. If it has led a wicked life, she pushes them from the road and allows it to fall into the Circle of Ghosts.

HUMANS: Mortal creatures without firsthand knowledge of the SPIRIT WORLD or SPIRITS.

INANOKA*: Mortal beings born of a human female and the SPIRIT TOB TOB. They are SKINWALKERS who shape-shift into the animal of their mother's tribe at will and maintain all attributes of that animal while in human form. They are called HALFLINGS and live an average of four hundred years. They are despised by NIYANOKA for being beasts and possibly because they live longer. They protect animals from capricious SUPERNATURALS. Each animal is gifted with a different power.

> **BEAR:** Has the ability to heal all injuries and wounds.

> **WOLF:** Can track anyone on earth by their scent trail.

> **RAVEN:** Is the only creature who can travel the Spirit Road and speak to the souls in the Spirit World.

BUFFALO: Is a creature of sacrifice that can absorb injuries, illness or grief into its body and then heal at a rapid rate. They are not healers and must feel all the pain they take from the one they relieve. It is said they can raise the dead, but only at the expense of their own life.

KANKA: Old woman sorceress. She travels in dreams and helps people purify themselves. She can see the past, present and future and is a SUPERNATURAL.

MAKA: Mother Earth, holds the female power of birth and is a sacred SPIRIT.

MITAKUYE OYASIN: A closing for a blessing. It literally means "All my relations included" or "We are all related" and reminds us that humans are connected to everything of the earth.

NAGI: This shadow creature is the ghostly guardian of the CIRCLE OF GHOSTS and is a SPIRIT.

NIYAN: SPIRIT BEING that teaches man to understand the cycle of life and death and the return of the body to MAKA (the earth) as the spirit returns to the SPIRIT WORLD. NIYAN is a SPIRIT.

NIYANOKA*: Mortal beings born of a union between NIYAN and a human. They are called SPIRIT CHILD and are charged with protecting humans from the interference of SUPERNATURALS and SKINWALKERS. In addition, they consider themselves shepherds of mankind, working for their benefit, helping them walk the RED ROAD and preparing them for the SPIRIT WORLD. They have a life span of 300 to 400 years.

PEACEMAKER*:   A NIYANOKA with the power to influence the moods and emotions of those nearby. They are highly persuasive and sought after for their ability to assist in all forms of negotiation. Since their suggestions are difficult to defy and their proposals hold such influence, their ethics must be above reproach.

RED ROAD: The RED ROAD is a metaphor for the correct way to live. One who walks the RED ROAD exists in balance with all things of the earth, behaving in a manner that is both proper and blessed.

SEER OF SOULS*:   A NIYANOKA member of the Ghost Clan, thought to be extinct. Such a HALFLING has the ability to see not only SPIRITS but earthbound souls in the form of disembodied GHOSTS. They have the power to speak to GHOSTS and to send them to the SPIRIT ROAD for judgment. See: Hihankara

SKINWALKERS: Another word for INANOKA, the Halfling children of TOB TOB, the SPIRIT bear. Legend says these are animals who remove their skin to masquerade as humans, but their ineptitude often reveals them.

SPIRITS: All these creatures are immortal.

SPIRIT CHILD*:   Another name for NIYANOKA, a HALFLING child of NIYAN and a human parent.

SPIRIT ROAD (SKY-ROAD, SPIRIT TRAIL, WAY OF SOULS):   The Milky Way that is the path leading to the SPIRIT WORLD. Those without the proper tattoos are pushed off the trail and wander endlessly in the CIRCLE OF GHOSTS. Souls without the proper markings have led an evil life on earth and do not merit entrance to the SPIRIT WORLD.

SPIRIT WORLD: The home of all ghosts that have successfully crossed the SPIRIT ROAD.

SUPERNATURALS: There are eight SUPER-NATURALs, including KANKA. They are immortal but less powerful than SPIRITS. They live on earth.

THE BALANCE: This refers to the balance of nature, the fragile connection which the LANOKA protect from careless or malevolent damage by supernatural creatures, NIYANOKA and HUMANS, who all tend to feel a certain entitlement to the earth.

TOB TOB: Translates as "Four by Four," meaning a creature that goes on four legs. This great SPIRIT bear has wisdom and healing powers. TOB TOB is a SPIRIT.

WANAGI: The soul of a dead person, a GHOST.

WAKAN TANKA: The Great Spirit, the Great Mystery, creator of all. A holy immortal entity who is more than SPIRIT.

WAKINYAN THUNDERBEINGS (THUNDERBIRD, THUNDERHORSE): The power of electric energy on earth. Lightning comes from the opening of the THUNDERBIRD's eyes and thunder from the beating of the THUNDERBIRD's wings and the drumming of the THUNDERHORSES' hooves. WAKINYA are SPIRITS. They also cause clouds, hurricanes, tornadoes and storms. They are known to strike dead any human foolish enough to lie while holding a sacred pipe.

WAY OF SOULS: (See SPIRIT ROAD)

WI: The sun. WI represents power and sustains life. He is a great teacher and a SPIRIT.

WONIYA: The soul of a living person.

---

* These terms/beings are fictional and do not exist in LAKOTA LEGEND.

nocturne™

COMING NEXT MONTH

Available May 31, 2011

#113 THE VAMPIRE WHO LOVED ME
Sons of Midnight
Theresa Meyers

#114 DÉJÀ VU
Lisa Childs

REQUEST YOUR FREE BOOKS!

2 FREE NOVELS PLUS 2 FREE GIFTS!

Harlequin®

nocturne™

Dramatic and Sensual Tales of Paranormal Romance.

YES! Please send me 2 FREE Harlequin® Nocturne™ novels and my 2 FREE gifts (gifts are worth about $10). After receiving them, if I don't wish to receive any more books, I can return the shipping statement marked "cancel." If I don't cancel, I will receive 4 brand-new novels every other month and be billed just $4.47 per book in the U.S. or $4.99 per book in Canada. That's a saving of at least 15% off the cover price! It's quite a bargain! Shipping and handling is just 50¢ per book in the U.S. and 75¢ per book in Canada.* I understand that accepting the 2 free books and gifts places me under no obligation to buy anything. I can always return a shipment and cancel at any time. Even if I never buy another book, the two free books and gifts are mine to keep forever.

238/338 HDN FC5T

Name	(PLEASE PRINT)

Address	Apt. #

City	State/Prov.	Zip/Postal Code

Signature (if under 18, a parent or guardian must sign)

Mail to the Reader Service:
IN U.S.A.: P.O. Box 1867, Buffalo, NY 14240-1867
IN CANADA: P.O. Box 609, Fort Erie, Ontario L2A 5X3

Not valid for current subscribers to Harlequin Nocturne books.

Want to try two free books from another line?
Call 1-800-873-8635 or visit www.ReaderService.com.

* Terms and prices subject to change without notice. Prices do not include applicable taxes. Sales tax applicable in N.Y. Canadian residents will be charged applicable taxes. Offer not valid in Quebec. This offer is limited to one order per household. All orders subject to credit approval. Credit or debit balances in a customer's account(s) may be offset by any other outstanding balance owed by or to the customer. Please allow 4 to 6 weeks for delivery. Offer available while quantities last.

Your Privacy—The Reader Service is committed to protecting your privacy. Our Privacy Policy is available online at www.ReaderService.com or upon request from the Reader Service.

We make a portion of our mailing list available to reputable third parties that offer products we believe may interest you. If you prefer that we not exchange your name with third parties, or if you wish to clarify or modify your communication preferences, please visit us at www.ReaderService.com/consumerschoice or write to us at Reader Service Preference Service, P.O. Box 9062, Buffalo, NY 14269. Include your complete name and address.

HN11

Harlequin® Blaze™ brings you
New York Times *and* USA TODAY *bestselling author*
Vicki Lewis Thompson with three new steamy titles
from the bestselling miniseries SONS OF CHANCE

Chance isn't just the last name of these rugged
Wyoming cowboys—it's their motto, too!

Read on for a sneak peek at the first title,
SHOULD'VE BEEN A COWBOY

Available June 2011 only from Harlequin® Blaze™.

"THANKS FOR NOT TURNING ON THE LIGHTS," Tyler said. "I'm a mess."

"Not in my book." Even in low light, Alex had a good view of her yellow shirt plastered to her body. It was all he could do not to reach for her, mud and all. But the next move needed to be hers, not his.

She slicked her wet hair back and squeezed some water out of the ends as she glanced upward. "I like the sound of the rain on a tin roof."

"Me, too."

She met his gaze briefly and looked away. "Where's the sink?"

"At the far end, beyond the last stall."

Tyler's running shoes squished as she walked down the aisle between the rows of stalls. She glanced sideways at Alex. "So how much of a cowboy are you these days? Do you ride the range and stuff?"

"I ride." He liked being able to say that. "Why?"

"Just wondered. Last summer, you were still a city boy. You even told me you weren't the cowboy type, but you're...different now."

He wasn't sure if that was a good thing or a bad thing. Maybe she preferred city boys to cowboys. "How am I different?"

"Well, you dress differently, and your hair's a little longer. Your face seems a little more chiseled, but maybe that's because of your hair. Also, there's something else, something harder to define, an attitude…"

"Are you saying I have an attitude?"

"Not in a bad way. It's more like a quiet confidence."

He was flattered, but still he had to laugh. "I just admitted a while ago that I have all kinds of doubts about this event tomorrow. That doesn't seem like quiet confidence to me."

"This isn't about your job, it's about…your…" She took a deep breath. "It's about your sex appeal, okay? I have no business talking about it, because it will only make me want to do things I shouldn't do." She started toward the end of the barn. "Now, where's that sink? We need to get cleaned up and go back to the house. Dinner is probably ready, and I—"

He spun her around and pulled her into his arms, mud and all. "Let's do those things." Then he kissed her, knowing that she would kiss him back, knowing that this time he would take that kiss where he wanted it to go. And she would let him.

Follow Tyler and Alex's wild adventures in
SHOULD'VE BEEN A COWBOY
Available June 2011 only from Harlequin® Blaze™
wherever books are sold.

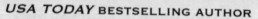